Tiffany Calvert *#416*

The Louisville Review
Summer/Fall 2024

95

The Louisville Review

Editor	Flora K. Schildknecht
Founding Editor	Sena Jeter Naslund
Guest Poetry Editor	Maureen Morehead
Guest Fiction Editor	Robin Lippincott
Cornerstone Editor	Betsy Woods
Managing Editor	Amy Foos Kapoor
Technical Director	Ron Schildknecht
Financial Director	John David Morgan

The Louisville Review publishes two volumes each year.
Visit our website for complete guidelines, back issues, subscriptions, and more: www.louisvillereview.org.

Follow us on Facebook for up-to-date information:
www.facebook.com/TheLouisvilleReview

Questions? Please note our email and mailing address:
associateeditor@louisvillereview.org

The Louisville Review
1436 St. James Court #1
Louisville, Kentucky 40208

This issue: $12 ppd
Sample copy: $6 ppd
Subscriptions: One year, $20; two years, $40; three years, $55.
Subscribers outside the United States please add $35/year for shipping.

Text and cover printed in the United States.
Cover and interior design by Jonathan Weinert.

Cover artwork, back cover detail: *#416*, oil on water based latex print on canvas, 22 x 28 inches, 2023. Photo by Mindy Best.

The Louisville Review is a not-for-profit publication.
The Louisville Review Corporation is a member of the Community of Literary Magazines and Presses.

© 2024 by The Louisville Review Corporation. All rights revert to the authors.

Editor's Note

For the cover of this **ninety-fifth** issue of *The Louisville Review* we are delighted to present a new painting, *#416*, by **Tiffany Calvert**. Past, present, and future collide in this work created in collaboration with Artificial Intelligence, and Calvert describes the ways in which historic Dutch and Flemish still life, machine learning, and original painterly gesture converge in her unique process in her statement on the work in our Nonfiction section.

Along with Calvert's innovative painting the poetry and prose in this issue demonstrate the necessity of the arts, especially during global uncertainty and divisive domestic politics. Reading *TLR* 95, I'm reminded of the power of the written word—to reveal injustice and suffering, but also to make visible efforts to protect and to nurture, to embolden us to hope that our gestures of goodwill might "be of some consequence after all," as **Julie Marie Wade** writes in her lyric essay featured in this issue.

We're proud to present new poems by **Jeanie Thompson** that address the brutalities of the U.S. immigration system and the aftermath of trauma, while also illuminating the redemptive qualities of poetry and art. Likewise, new poems by **Wille Carver Jr.** engage the scourges of opioid addiction and homophobia, while also testifying to the enduring love and agency of our animal companions. Short fiction from **Gregory Byrd** envisions the aftermath of the massacre of an African American town in Jim Crow Florida, while short fiction from **E. Reid** celebrates two women's joyful creation of a new family in Tennessee. Looking beyond the United States, readers will encounter something of family life in Guatemala, and of life in the long shadow of war in Bosnia, in short fiction by **Emilio Gomez** and **Katya Cengel**, respectively.

Since 1976, *The Louisville Review* has operated as a journal where established and emerging writers are published side by side. Today, I like to think of *The Louisville Review* as an extended community of writers and readers, and in these pages, we welcome returning contributors **Lennie Hay**, **Marcia L. Hurlow**, **Pat Owen**, and **Robert Sachs**, as well as new contributors **Stephen D. Abney**, **Thomas Dukes**,

Arva Elliot, Ilan Mochari, Jesse Mountjoy, Dana Murphy, Madari Pendas, Lizzy Ke Polishan, Margaret Rozga, Caris Uşoară, Whitney Vale, and S.E. Wilson, to name just a few.

The work we do at *TLR* would not be possible without the vital efforts of our guest genre editors, and it's been my pleasure to work on this issue with two authors who have been steadfast supporters of *The Louisville Review* over the years. I extend heartfelt thanks to our returning Guest Poetry Editor, who, along with myself, selected the poetry for this issue:

Maureen Morehead is a retired teacher from Jefferson County Schools. She was on the poetry faculty in the Naslund-Mann Graduate School of Writing at Spalding University. She's published poems in many literary magazines including *American Poetry Review*, *American Voice*, *The Kenyon Review Online*, *The Louisville Review*, and *Poetry*. She's also published six books of poetry, four by Gray Zeitz of Larkspur Press. The most recent is *The Red Gate*. She served as the 2011-2012 Kentucky Poet Laureate.

Likewise, I must extend deep gratitude to our returning Guest Fiction Editor, who, along with Founding Editor **Sena Jeter Naslund**, selected the fiction for this issue:

Robin Lippincott is the author of six books, most recently *Blue Territory: A Meditation on the Life and Art of Joan Mitchell*. His fiction, nonfiction, and poetry have appeared in *The Paris Review*, *Fence*, *American Short Fiction*, *Diode*, *The New York Times Book Review*, and many other journals. He teaches in the MFA Program of the Naslund-Mann Graduate School of Writing at Spalding University.

And, to **Betsy Woods**, Editor of Cornerstone, *The Louisville Review*'s section featuring poetry by young writers in grades K-12, sincere thanks for all you do to lift up and promote the work of the next generation of writers.

—Flora K. Schildknecht, Editor

Table of Contents

Poetry

Jesse Mountjoy	Plowing with Vernon	3
Pamela Wax	Shea Stadium, 1972	4
Eric Weil	Barred Owl Livestream	6
Gregory Byrd	At Assisted Living, the Botanist Recognizes an Old Love	8
Lennie Hay	Drowning While Reading Seamus Heaney	9
Lizzy Ke Polishan	luther burbank took his potato-patent cash & booked a train to santa rosa	11
Avra Elliot	In Monsoon Season, the Desert Amphibians Wake	13
Nan Byrne	Train from Paris	14
Whitney Vale	At the Mystic Motel	15
Clare Kramer	Inheritance	16
Marcia L. Hurlow	A Blues for the Pandemic	18
Jeanie Thompson	1979: The Child Who Drew a Map of His Country	19
	Ode to a Brownie Scout Dress	21
	Her Hair	23
	Request to Mrs. Mary Ann Pettway of Gee's Bend, Alabama, To Transform a Dress into a Quilt	25
Margaret Rozga	Yellow	27
Caris Uşoară	My belly a buzzing ting	28

Pat Owen	Polishing My Shoes	29
Virginia Lee Alcott	Old Windows	31
Dana Murphy	Intergenerational Violets	32
Karl Plank	Clarity	34
Madari Pendas	In Your Next Life	35
Mark Madigan	One Love	36
Mary Ellen Talley	Still Life with Tomatoes	38
Abigail Byrd-Stapleton	News	39
Wille Carver Jr.	Narcotic Genealogy	41
	Lucy. A Witness.	43
	Turbulence is Expected	44
Ron Hickerson	Intro to Newswriting	46
Thomas Dukes	Driveway Lilies	48
Angie Macri	Witchgrass,	49
Kelly Granito	Spring	50
	Goodbye	51
Alex Green	Beach State Inventory	52
Christy Prahl	The Grocery Pageant	53
Kara Lewis	The Definition of Fermentation	55
Grace Bauer	When She Was Only Anna	57
Camille Hernandez	aunty culture, part 3	59
Ellen Wright	Where Old Easter Lilies Go to Die	61

Nonfiction

Tiffany Calvert	Artist's Statement, *#416*	65
Julie Marie Wade	Four Altars	67

Fiction

Gregory Byrd	Boy Abducted by Bear	79
Robert Sachs	Wary	90
Emilio Gomez	La Quema del Diablo	94
E. Reid	The Holy Family	99
Ilan Mochari	Shirley's Sticky Sole (1982)	110
Katya Cengel	A Palm Tree in the Ruins	114
S.E. Wilson	The Ranch	126
Stephen D. Abney	Frog Bottoms: Hannah's Birthday	133

Cornerstone

Erika Prasthofer	Poetic Reserve	139
Jack DeBoyace	Deterioration, They Said	140
	Valley	141
Pharaoh Jones	Manicured Forest	142
	Cabbage and Cantaloupe	143
Adebola Adenle	Interphase	145
Jovina Zion Pradeep	Caramelized Marble	146

Sophie Watson	Resentment	148
	Amy	150
Clara Dekker	Iron Oxide	151
Eva Alcaraz-Monje	Appalachia is Contagious	152

Contributors' Notes	155
Cornerstone Contributor's Notes	163

Poetry

Jesse Mountjoy

Plowing with Vernon

The shape of the work. His mind
Moves with each shift of the mule's

Haunches in front of him. The earth's
Unravelments lie curled behind.

And each time at the end of a row
The mule chuffs and brays, his one

Rheumy eye swallowing the loose
Ends of the day. With the interaural

Capture of 'gee' and 'haw,' the mule
Changes places with Vernon who

Now, in this limitless field and time,
Pulls the plow, while the mule guides,

Measuring a straight row with
Uncanny powers of discernment.

They trudge on in the general vicinity
Of work, shifting from sad to mad, with

A stop or two at lazy. The shape of
Life walking back the length of the day.

Pamela Wax

Shea Stadium, 1972

      the vendors hawked Rheingold and peanuts
when one hollered *Beeya heeya*
    my father echoed *This is the place*
              and swapped cups from the tray
                    for a wad of bills
          Keep the change
    then passed the beer
           to the veterans of Post 146 in the seats around us
family friends with whom we'd shared a rented bus
      from the Jersey suburbs
    pooled bets on which inning
        would score the most runs
               and how Yogi might fare as the new manager

I asked about the black armbands on the left sleeves
            of the uniforms
    my father ran on about honoring the death of a comrade
      the old manager who'd dropped dead

          I was twelve   and gawky
    hid puberty under layers of oversize
      marveled at my father's largesse
    dispensing dollars just like that
But Dad when he handed me a twenty to go buy 30
    40-cent knishes   *Keep the change*
      it's only money
and I didn't understand the *only* then
or that *this is*
         the place   right here

                         now   and how dozing on the bus ride home
after the Mets beat the Pirates
        I overheard pride
                when he mentioned my good grades
how I'd amount to something
        not have to stand on my feet
                for twelve hours a day

        my father who reclined on Sundays with WQXR
blasting all classical
                a red and white can of Rheingold by his side
        as he scanned the yard through binoculars
consulting his Peterson field guide only when an enigma
                breezed in for a landing

        my father who hid *The Joy of Sex*
right next to the encrypted Masonic handbook
                in his nightstand where he thought
        I'd never find them

                my father who didn't want to know
I was blooming under my layers
                        almost ready to decipher adult mysteries
                like loyalty to comrades
                        or generosity to those who aren't blood

Eric Weil

Barred Owl Livestream

Barred owls roost in the easement protecting
the creek that divides our suburban street
from another, where someone built a big
nesting box and installed a camera
that spies on their nightly activities.
The nest isn't much: a few twigs and leaves,
a little moss, thin layer on the floor
like litter, while we imagine for ourselves
trendy upgrades we watch on TV: shiplap,
"Open Concept," new hardwood floors,
whether to sell or stay. The night-
sensitive camera picks up the male
as he lands on the box lip, wings
outspread, offering a mouse to his mate.
She accepts, moves only an inch. Surely
she warms eggs under her downy belly.
He goes, returns in minutes, another
mouse. Mouse after mouse, most nights, literal
fast food. Once, perhaps tired of the menu,
she leaves the box and nabs a baby rabbit.
Under three minutes. The livestream lifts us
out of our daily habitual consumption:
Starbucks, Amazon, Target. We
admire devotion to the next generation
while comparing online therapies for feelings
of inadequacy, work stress. The male
brings another mouse, but the mothers
of small children are wary. Last year's owl
laid two eggs. One hatched and the hatchling died,
featherless as a chunk of raw chicken

on a cutting board. The other egg might
as well have been a stone. Trauma among
toddlers when the owls disappeared. But
they, apparently the same owl couple,
came back this spring, began again. The moms
pray for the owls' success, warning
their kids that while Nature provides
many mice, not all owlets become owls.
After a delivery, the male turns
to gaze into the night before gliding
away on patrol, to feed whatever
the future holds, while we watch, thankful
for internet connections in our warm rooms
lit by quivering rectangular screens.

Gregory Byrd

At Assisted Living, the Botanist Recognizes an Old Love

What if it was really the way we thought it was
all those years ago?
What if the silver desire for lips and arched backs
the flower blooming on the tip of a mango branch,
and scent and soft folds tipped with morning dew
was really the promise of a long-nourishing fruit
instead of only a flash of color and smell
for fluttering wings.

And if, all these years later, we recognize the fruit
first, and the blossom as the titillating promise,
do we eat only the sweet yellow slices
with lime, the flesh of fiber and vitamins
and hint now, with a smile in a sunny chair
a grey eye aged by loss, how the flower would have felt
on a morning when all was quiet but us,
before our wings had carried us to other blooms.

Lennie Hay

Drowning While Reading Seamus Heaney

Before I knew *Bone Dreams*, heard *Bann Clay*
we slogged a Northern Indiana bog.
Oversized waders made suction cup
feet. They stuttered and I fell.
Wet jean anchor pulled
me thick into layers of leaves,
fossils, inside an earth conquering earth,
memories of lost stags
caught in Northern winters.

We trudged, listened to how dead years
spawn new life; a local naturalist
talked of this sweet ground
where we stood while we sank
inch by inch, thinking of how living matter pickles
everything in these conditions.
We stood in awe
while fungi worked to make a quagmire.

Today I read his poems,
inch by inch. Remember that wet walk.
A soggy music makes more melody
each day. His stew of dead berries,
resurrected bones suck my brain.
I follow the lines through lough
and broagh, and Toome. Relish Anahorish.
Fold his mother's sheets with him.
Sweat over *Digging*. Gasp. Inhale
familiar words, find a tool to forge meaning
with a plough and spade. I gaze
on haw fruit, Bann River's divide.

I touch *bell-notes, water-blistered cornfields,*
feel accents strike accents.

His endless Ireland less strange now;
underwater I read a bubbling brilliance.

Lizzy Ke Polishan

luther burbank took his potato-patent cash & booked a train to santa rosa

  back when marie was skłodowska

& when i tell you she was snatched i mean did she do all that science in a corset cause girl

  i was already impressed that's love, i guess, like that ancient mausoleum

with 36 pillars & 25 steps & a chariot on top & art, from 4 greek

  masters, that the dead beloved would never see but that's love i guess we never know

if we see what our lover wants us to see our lover, or anyone, really

  i often think of the time sartre got a haircut baby

sarte got a haircut   he had these gorgeous

  golden curls, then he didn't anymore & his mother screamed

& called him a toad & he didn't understand . . . i want to know how many times

  we talk about chopin without talking about george sand, & how many times

we talk about george sand without mentioning her many famous lovers it doesn't seem fair

  that radium gets all the credit when polonium was named for a homeland

still i want to see radium-kissed fingers cracked to silver rivers

i want to see   the hole in pierre's chest   i want to
    know   marie

when you gave all those elements names   how shallow was your
    laced breath

Avra Elliott

In Monsoon Season, the Desert Amphibians Wake

And where we said it should be casual,
a toad of affection appears. *Don't text me
Don't talk to me.* Unless it is to arrange
when we meet, to jokingly praise nature by being
bare together under the rain and hot skies.
And this agreement lasts less than a day
because we make the mistake of exchanging
playlists and I hear a Johnny Cash song that makes me
think of and text him, and he brings me stones he thinks I'd like.
And so we plan something violent,
something to soothe the desires true crime shows breed,
but the shed he's thrown a mattress in is pretty in afternoon light,
and with my control removed,
I am fast to change my mind, and he is quick to soothe me,
so we fucking cuddle, which is not ideal, and we talk
about our kids and our aging parents. He asks if I am sure
I don't need love or commitment. I say I don't need
commitment, and I don't require the other to enjoy
the rain on my face and the pleasure of other bodies,
but we don't believe each other, not quite, so I lie by truth
I say, yes, I want you to love me. I demand a thousand dead toads
as a sign of your devotion. He says to wait a moment, and I am content
to have driven him away, to outstrange the stranger—
but he sends a thousand and a couple hundred extra
cartoon frogs to my phone.
They aren't dead, I say. *You don't love me*, I quietly imply.
They aren't alive, he says, and we listen to the croaks
that call from droughted ground.

Nan Byrne

Train from Paris

We stood on the platform in Paris talking
Exhausted travelers visiting with sons and daughters
Behind us the great gray engines were snorting in rows
as we chatted about deeds that should not have been done
Many years ago, should not have been remembered then
and all the time our train was ready to go. Hidden fully
at the back of the pack. Above us words drained from the speaker
into a spaghetti of sound. If this had been Italy we might have understood
but this was France and we were speaking of weakness, a thing
that keeps a person cemented in place for years. When I felt
a slight movement inside me, a desire truly to escape
Grabbing my bag I pulled myself off to the side and ran
I ran until my chest hurt. I ran toward that dark thing waiting
Leaving behind you, my children, leaving behind our journey
I climbed aboard the train and somehow you were there beside me
heaving our suitcases into a space. Sitting on a seat like a king
your shoes untied. They will never catch us, you said.

Whitney Vale

At the Mystic Motel,

a vending machine's trays hold soda pop, cheese crackers, condoms
and rabbit feet—feeling lucky? My room is number 12, always
an auspicious number for me. The cream-colored pillow with its
embroidered eye placed in the middle of the bed wards off bad vibes.
So does the double lock. The gift shop in reception holds oracle cards
and palo santo bundles. Tote bags to hold useless metaphors cost
more than your breakfast. And yet you ache for one. Ravens cough
black noise from the desert shrubs, and I look for heart shaped stones,
always a dreamer. Always on a quest to deny the dry moss in my guts.
Corralled horses trot to the fence and want to stick their muzzles
and yellow teeth in my pockets. I am all out of sweet, but they must
smell the echo of an earlier me, maybe they smell my inner child, that
tiresome symbol, that wanton popsicle.

Clare Kramer

Inheritance

for my grandmother

she came from raised voice
    & locked door
        Pennsylvania winters that chip away
            a little more each year,
from *the red red robin*
    & "You'll never make it
    as a writer"
from baby on each hip
    & dissolving
        ambitions
    hard cool of well water on the skin
from blackbirds
        exploding up from frozen
    fields
she came from
    bluegrass, from dirt
    under fingernails
from white hallways & folded
    sheets, incandescent lights,
    visiting hours at Our Lady
        of Peace
she came from
    kids in bed & "Hello, Dolly"

    she walks from the house to
the garden, to the bank of the
pond, and her heart
    drags behind
        her

   and her feet never touch
the ground

she came from late-night
  rosaries, from the way
  moonlight slips
    across the bedroom wall
she came from
  the belt
  & the liquor
from hospitals & cherry blossoms
  from the front porch swing
    the doctor's daughter
she came from dead stars
  like us all

Winner of the 2023/24 Annette Allen Poetry Prize, Julie Marie Wade, Judge

Marcia L. Hurlow

A Blues for the Pandemic

I leave room for mistakes. I leave
this room to find another way
to start to start. For two years now
I've hardly left the house, opened
the door to retrieve what is left
and what is left looks gray, looks
like what I must pack in the room
for non-perishables. I'm perishing.
Peanut butter collects between tines
of forks, bananas collect dots
of sugar to melt in the bread I bake
and take to the room where we eat
that day, the feast that floats
from the kitchen to the living room,
the back deck, the porch, what
passes for travel. The dog
finds a field to run in. I herd him
from other people who found
the same field. We leave room.
They leave room. We wave
away their greetings and return.

Jeanie Thompson

1979: The Child Who Drew a Map of His Country

Dear James, I asked you to write to me
                      about what is in your heart.
For me, I carried mine around like a shirt
                      I wanted to wear
that was way too big,
                      how would
I put it on? Like boots I wanted
                      to step into
but my feet knew
                      they would pinch, bind, sear.
How could I tell
                      what I was feeling in a way
that added anything
                      to the conversation?
The idea, the pain—
                      and then in the streaming footage
of caged children at the border, I saw one boy
                      sitting by himself,
surrounded by others on the bench,
                      but he was alone, holding on
to his dignity, managing his fear,
                      and I remembered
Jose, the five-year-old in Summer in the City,
                      in poetry class, in New Orleans,
It was 1979.
                      "Hello Misses Jeanie," he would say
in hearty greeting.
                      Working together at his table,
happy that such a young person was interested
                      in poetry, at ease with a stranger,
I asked him where he was from

                    and he said, "El Savador,
Do you know … ?"
                    and he drew a map of his country,
accurate, like the map of his home
                    was blazing in his head.
His small fingers expertly
                    moving the pencil
and later he would write poems,
                    which I know I will tear
into my ancient files to find
                    like a mother
seeking a lost one's favorite blanket.
                    I was younger then,
much younger, injured,
                    no child of my own.
I loved Jose with an outsized love
                    which I knew was wrong
but it didn't matter.
                    He wrote a poem, I know it is still out there.
He was one child, in one place,
                    who stays with me.
Because of how we met,
                    but more than that.
I knew nothing of his family,
                    his status, his future, but he was
safe enough in the USA to attend
                    the summer camp, to write poems,
to make music,
                    to draw a map of his country
for a woman who grieved
                    her own grief, and was comforted
by the magnificent,
                    fearless light of his face.

Jeanie Thompson

Ode to a Brownie Scout Dress

Packed into a plastic bin marked *winter*
there you are. How can I release you?
You emerge like a photo in a chemical bath,
a folded moment taking shape.
Small brown dress of my fourth-grade year,
you reappear, packed, unpacked, repacked.
He stood in the doorway, light behind him –
it was the middle of the night.
Someone I knew betrayed me, startled me
awake, something out of place, but vivid.
It had been Brownie Scout Day,
I had worn you, my pride –
I tried to shield my eyes with my arm,
but he moved my arm.
Unpacked me so I would see.
Mother and Dad had gone somewhere, left us
with neighbors. Trusted friends.
It was the middle of the night.
Where was brother?
Just the young man alone,
silhouetted in the bedroom door.
Years later the memory unpacked itself,
I remembered he looked at his hand.
Though I packed this memory deep you reappear,
an indictment of my silent younger self.
A small brown dress,
unadorned, no badges,
the seams, buttons, the hemline,
the little collar and set-in sleeves.
How beautifully you were made,

someone made you with care,
My mother bought you.
I believe that little girl who wore you,
her innocent pride.
She packed you, unpacks you
cannot let you go.

Jeanie Thompson

Her Hair

On that last day
that I did not know would be

a last day, I touched your hair, your prize,
matted, unwashed, the silver curls

springy with what we call *body*, as your ninety pounds
clung to the bed rail and you moaned

for water. I tried to comfort by
stroking your hair – fully

aware of what I was doing, and that your
brilliant brain, acerbic quips, terror

were there beneath my touch.
I splayed my fingers

and cupped your whole head,
entangling as a daughter can, my

dumb fingers in your hair. If my touch
on your skull spoke anything to you

I can't know.
Something sat on my shoulder

and whispered *do this*.
Later, at the place where questions

seemed to walk up to me, the woman said,
Do you want a lock of hair?

Yes, I said,
yes, two.

At Christmas
I took the robust silver

And deep brown curls from the small
Plastic bag, tied them with silk ribbon,

placed each in a small box for
two nieces. Closest girl children. I knew

I wasn't doing this right, that they wouldn't
know the right way either, but I wanted

to pass that hair to someone who had
touched you.

In the bag I still keep
a lock for myself. I open it and inhale

the faint scent of you, almost gone.
But that hair!

Wonderfully vibrant – calls to me,
will not be burned.

Jeanie Thompson

Request to Mrs. Mary Ann Pettway of Gee's Bend, Alabama, to Transform a Dress into a Quilt

Because I have visited your collective and have seen the strips
of fabric, pieces of workers' clothes, an athlete's jerseys,
homemade items transformed into patterns that soothe and bring joy,
I make this bold request.

Can you help me free the pain
that resides in a small brown dress?
I have tried to write it out, but it will not budge.

Can you unsew the collar? Unset the sleeves? Unplacket
the buttonholes? Release the hem and let it wave like a flag?

Can you clip the buttons and transform
them to stones from the river, the center of a sunflower?

With your sharp shears I know you can cut
and unpattern the dress, lay it out
as a diamond, a starburst, a housetop,
a miracle beyond a small girl's shattered dream.

See what the dress might release, as you saw
what those worn work shirts, faded jeans would tell.

Can you unpin the Brownie, that dancing sprite,
from the pocket, and gather the numbers from the sleeve
to add up to a path back to innocence?

I trust your keen eye and discerning heart
to set this dress ablaze in dream, free of memory,
to an abstraction in brown and white, beyond pain.

Thank you for letting me ask after I have made my way
across the river on the ferry, where you said *the trees shimmer silver,
lighter green, darker green, greenest green* in Gee's Bend.

Note: Lines in italics are from the PBS documentary, *Quiltmakers of Gee's Bend.*

Margaret Rozga

Yellow

Tell me, if you can,
how in this world
bright with the glorious
height of coneflower,
cup plant, and goldenrod,
yellow became the name
for the shame of cowardice.

Walk this August prairie with me.
Let's see what's in bloom, savor
five, eight, thirteen, twenty-
petalled proclamations of life that,
however briefly, stand tall with
what let's call the color of courage.

Caris Uşoară

My belly a buzzing ting

You have placed yourself in long loops, coiled with the dog, near me making a nest, Ordinary Sunday dawn. The dampness locks the little bones all in me, pulls them tight, serrated like piano wire and out of sight, those facet knuckles all along my spine. The little knots in my hands, my feet, get all bogged in. In our loose furls and tight bonds, warm slow breaths hum, mixing, we make vapor. My lungs let out low sighs, my belly a buzzing ting. Moving away, moving toward, oscillating sway.

Pat Owen

Polishing my Shoes

In my lifetime
two people have polished my shoes
unsolicited
just because it needed doing
and they loved me.

But today it's just me
doing what needs to be done,
my black clogs worn almost daily
now neglected and scuffed.

I find the shoeshine bag
unused for years
still carrying its life-long accumulations—
polishes in oxblood, tan and black—
cans pried opened by a penny—
oily scent I remember from childhood.

Just as years ago,
I dump the bag's contents
onto old newspaper on the floor,
set aside the yellow saddle soap
and the black polish,
a wood -handled brush and a soft cloth.

In honor of my father,
who showed me how
I clean, polish, brush,
and shine with an old cotton tee shirt.

I'm playing the part
of those who loved me,
who showed me how to love.

Virginia Lee Alcott

Old Windows

The day they replaced the old windows in the house,
she said to put them in the back yard with
thoughts of transforming them into pieces of art.

Months went by like the local train, and the windows, poised
in their slanted pile grew with
grass and jewel weed cramming every crack.

Moss crept along each pane as if brush stroked in
green accent over the rain splashed mud. Pieces of
birch bark and cedar branches drizzled along the edges.

The occasional wren perched on an edge as it gaged
its surroundings, unperturbed by the unusual structure
in the midst of lilac bushes and an aged hedgerow.

In summer she sat on the porch swing and nodded
towards the sculpture of windows, contemplating
on a future project or ethereal transformation.

She maneuvered around the windows as she
tended to the yard, in no rush to change the slant
of the pile or move one window into the open.

Winter snows hid everything so that only the
bird prints ran across the top. A cold embrace
promising to insulate the secrets once denied.

Dana Murphy

Intergenerational Violets

It smells so nice in here
a woman's voice enters my office,
layered with another's.

A third is sitting in the pulse points
under my wrists slathering me in
baby powder and *Royal Violets* so
I smell nice for our bus ride to the mall
to take photos where I would only
cry out for my mother instead.

*Although this was not the news
you were expecting* they have never been
in my office before. Perhaps they expected
it to smell bad

like Neutrogena, teen magazines,
and being bullied online,
before she took the thirty-mile bus ride
from South Gate to our tree-lined street to stay,
the overwhelming florals of her exile
from one country and my erasure in
another intertwining

in the ongoing olfactory of
new Jim Crow and no way out.
Not even to breathe in my office with
my door closed, my great-aunt stuck
in the ventilation,
remembering Cuba as violets.

I wondered what the women before me
smelled like under the J.Crew of their
blazers, light blue shirts, and skinny jeans.

I can't be human right now
I can't be human right now
I can't be human right now
one kept repeating, the other looking
for an empty space for her eyes.

Karl Plank

Clarity

> *after Georgia O'Keeffe's* White Canadian Barn II, 1932

We would have clarity
like the clean lines of a northern barn,
low and long, single-minded in devotion
to form's function.
We might shelter here.
Plain white walls,
broken by few, dark rectangles
resist any grave complication.
Simplicity is a clean face.
Lucidity, shut entries and a roof of midnight.
Yet, someone left ajar
the small stable door at the end,
as if he intended to return from a brief chore.
I'll be right back, he explains to his creatures,
stalled, languid for right now.
He has been called away, we think,
but has not come home,
the reasons not clear at all.

Madari Pendas

In Your Next Life

come back as a bee, something with a stinger or horn or that shoots venom through spikes
remember when you used to imagine you could choose what you'd become?

> Human as stasis
> temporary
> preamble

you could be both boy and girl and neither   when you drew stripes across your hands
predator   trying to blend into the brambles   you filed your nails into points, summits at the ends of your fingers

Come back as

> a word with a lot of Rs
> as the sound of eyelashes fluttering together
> as a scar that migrates across an aging face

You used to say you were a boy   loving how the word itself made your lips squeeze, a kiss before release

remember how you stopped saying it once no one took you seriously
So you didn't either. What's a feeling anyways   What kind of woman would you be if you didn't hate being a woman

Come back as

> a fish that never falls for lures
> a flower with an uncertain bloom
> as a mandible that can bite through all flesh

Mark Madigan

One Love

Of all the great art
I saw on my first
visit to Florence—

whether ambling alone
through the Bargello,
or following others

through the long halls
of the Uffizi,
or staring, in awe,

at Michelangelo's
statue of David—
the memory that still

brings a broad smile back
was my last evening,
slowly traipsing

home after dinner,
when I stood a few moments
listening to a young man

playing guitar
and singing for spare change,
the hungry mouth

of his guitar case
propped open and showing
just a few coins.

Yet his clear voice
was filled with such a force
of joy and hope

that I couldn't help—
as he sang one
of my favorite songs

while a sleepy sun settled
off to the west—
but toss my loose change

into his case
as I started singing
that wonderful reggae

song to myself,
every glorious step
I took going home.

Mary Ellen Talley

Still Life with Tomatoes

Cezanne selected
nine large tomatoes
at Pike Place Market
from a stall
that doesn't raise prices
for the tourists.
He took the elevator
to his fifth-floor studio,
held the reds under the faucet
to feast on color,
then knifed each globe in half
on the maple board,
set the crimsons flat side up,
stirred a persillade
of chopped garlic and parsley,
spooned breadcrumbs,
layered extra olive oil
as Madame Renoir had suggested,
then baked the scarlet beauties
until serving his bearded associate.
They admired dusk setting in
amid chiaroscuros and city lights
outside the window,
discussed their plein air fascination
tasted bite by bite
and circled crusty bread in juices,
brushed the air with words
half noticing the strokes of time
that made them hurry.

Abigail Byrd-Stapleton

News

A thousand birds die in a single night,
breaking their small bodies on shining buildings,
drawn and confused by the synthetic city starlight.
Sometimes the metaphor resists itself, and you are left
holding a live grenade. Volunteers
scoop fractured-neck-broken-winged things
into industrial black trash bags
for days.

Meanwhile, two grown men hold each other in an embrace
as the last kindness either of them will know,
the turbine beneath their feet caught aflame. Rumors say
there was repelling equipment enough for one, and neither
could stomach leaving the other to face the blaze alone.
I don't know which parts are true, but two grown men
held each other tightly before dying– this much we know.

My brother works salvage diving and marina repair—
he says diving and space exploration are some of the only fields
we launched men out into the unknown, just to test the human limits.
He says the best way to sink a listing ship and save the dock is six men
with six knives, sawing in unison.

Starved and burnt bodies in bags wrack up like cigarettes
on my feed. The number of children in a given area
dwindles. I quit smoking in the spring and my chest feels
wetter than ever. A woman I used to barely understand
calls me every week while she gets dressed for work.
I help her choose her lipstick and she
tells me about her dying relatives, her new boyfriend,

and I briefly wish I had loved her more
when she was within arms reach of me.

I grow a child almost five thousand miles
from my loved ones. I plan on naming him
after the summer and water, and wonder what he will be
when he is grown; the broken indigo bunting,
or the man who leaves the skyscraper lights on.

Willie Carver Jr.

Narcotic Genealogy

The first time
my older brother overdosed
I was twelve and playing Zelda
the deep pulp of his neck muscles
bulged out and twisted around like
panicked roots growing upside down
paralyzed in their reach
for nonexistent dirt

I tried to find the sword
hidden by the forest mist
but kept losing my way

The first time
my younger sister overdosed
I was twenty and drove us to the ER
my dad dropped her bluing body
in the winter flakes of daybreak flurry
a wingless snow angel formed
we tread on it and broke
my mother's back in frost
splintering through time

I tried to drive the flailing car
over dead ice halted above concrete
but crashed into a fence

The first time
        you overdose,
one of my loved nephews,

it won't really be the first
the new covenant already sealed
the firmament still as wet
as prescription pad ink writing
down dreams until they thicken
into septic soil that levels hills

I will try scripture and politics
till they crumble in my hands
and reveal all our lucid sores

Willie Carver Jr.

Lucy. A Witness.

we carried you
for seventeen years
in and out the house
in a gray plastic carrier
with a metal barred door
but that final day out
on the way to end your life
I noticed then the first time
the watery sway of sunshine
bounce across its gated bars
your eyes replying to the light
that tore itself in living splendor
across 93,000,000 miles of sky
eight and a half glorious minutes
free of a five billion-year-old star
before collapsing into your eyes
that took in the photons
and saw a living world

Willie Carver Jr.

Turbulence is Expected

she gave me the window seat
laced her two truant buckles
flinched as carry-ons pinched
and coughed across Economy

she closed her eyes
I opened my book
I slid a thick pen
over sick statistics
of queer youth suicide
to prepare my talk

the plane ripped itself
from the skin of the earth
and I wondered if exposed
wounds heal faster

the cabin recoiled
and palsied winds
beat its ingot back
we shook together
and her jumping palm
clasped onto my leg

—Are you okay?
—Oh, God. I'm sorry. I'm a nervous flyer. I reached out and my heart was expecting my husband.
—It's okay. I don't fly well either. Would it help if we talked?
—Please. Thank you.
—Where are you going today, ma'am? Somewhere nice?

—A religious summit in Texas. We're hearing Jimmy Swaggart talk about how to fight back against this gay indoctrination and save our children.

the winds glowered
cabin air drizzled
hissed across us
then held its breath

—What about you, young man? Going to Texas?
—No. I have a layover. I'm going to an education conference in Florida. I will be speaking to education leaders about how to save LGBTQ youth from religious extremists.

her hands swooped in
one holding the other
the cabin air burst back
into the space we shared
the winds looked away
ink leached into my skin
and we seethed together

a current panted
hot against the wings
I noted in margins
she traced in tight rounds
her taught seat belt rosary
and washed dead oxygen
with wax paper prayer

I turned to her
—Ma'am. Do you have friends or family going with you on this trip?

Ron Hickerson

Intro to Newswriting

I thought of you today.
I thought of how you taught me words
Are important, so choose
Them carefully - not cautiously,
But full of care for a
Words' beauty or weight. I thought of
How you made us read poetry
And science fiction when
We were just learning to report
The news, making tutors of Wells
And Williams in Strunk and
White's classroom. I thought of how you
Taught us to make our words
Dance in time to AP style,
With concrete steps and light
Flourishes with every call. I
Wondered what you would think
Of my words today - If you would
Say I use the same words
Too much, or that I use abstruse
Vocabulary to
Obfuscate my meaning, or that
I pick easy words and
Insult readers' intelligence.
I hoped you would look at
My words like you looked at me in
Your office: under the
Stony stare of Jefferson's bust,
You smiled and told me
You never fretted about what

I'd write, then grabbed a page of saved
Newsprint with my byline
And said, "This is a good story."

Thomas Dukes

Driveway Lilies

I understand:
The long promise in your bud,
The once-in-a-day bloom,
Then, the end—
There are no third acts in lily lives.

You are a dream, the way
Tuscany is or a winter garden.
Perhaps that is why Rich
Grows you in breezy profusion,
Wild ballgowns of orange, dancing.

You are poisonous to cats.
I get it: divas seldom like each other.
Maria Callas didn't last long either,
But like you, she settled for
Being loved by all, and legend.

We can be short on magic in Ohio.
Still, we have our tricks:
Forest roses, wooly cattails
Rising from a ditch, and you
With a sense of the ending

We share today.

Angie Macri

Witchgrass,

a kind of panic grass, got its name
not from worry,
that god and the moods he brought,
but from the panicle,
its form, like a fountain of grain,
from the base word for bread.
Each house must have a good broom.
A witch would have the best,
and thus the name. A witch
would pay no attention to a god
and his feelings. She'd sweep her floor clean
of hair that fell, of crumbs and skin
we lose every day. She'd keep
her yard clean as well, old-fashioned space
of packed clay.
Who hadn't mounted a broomstick
just once to see?
What child didn't feed stick horses
made from old broomsticks,
knowing they could fly?
We stroked their sides as we rode through bedrooms,
yards, clouds, stars.
The woods made their noise,
and we never ran away.

Kelly Granito

Spring

Truth is, I don't care for gardening. I'm no Mary
quite contrary with her silver sea oddities
lined up in the dirt. I just like watching you
do it—run the wheelbarrow here and there, run your hands
over the milkweed, kneel to the earth to deadhead
the roses. Come summertime, come autumn leaves,
come winter's stabbing moon . . . Spring comes as easily
as I fall back in love, bringing certain rains that coax us
into bloom.

Kelly Granito

Goodbye

We reach for each other
with the obliquity of two sugar pines
that reach for the sky: stalwarts
of old growth, secretly slanting
into whatever path offers
each the clearest view
of the sun.

We forget
our braided, hairlike
roots will keep us
forever in cahoots,
while in the breeze we wave
a wordless, years-long
goodbye.

Alex Green

Beach State Inventory

The week of the Surf City Championships the competition announces it has an official hard cider. It comes in a gold bottle with a label featuring a drawing of a man in a spacesuit playing a wood instrument that's on fire. Originally the design had him surrounded by an audience of dancing aliens, but the CEO of the company delivered a late night memo that kept them off the bottle. *I think we've taken this far enough*, he wrote. At a reception in the hills, complimentary glasses are served by well-dressed young people holding trays shaped like surfboards while the Midnight Stability Orchestra plays outside on the patio. The wolf expert from the North ends up drinking too much and later that night writes a letter to someone she shouldn't and drops it in the mailbox in front of Porpoise's House of Pizza. The metal box is covered in coats of stickers of bands and businesses that no longer exist; on the side someone has carved: *You're terrible at being a person.* In the darkness of his hotel room, the surfer from San Diego tells the librarian's daughter about the time he drowned and was dead for eleven minutes. He tells her dying was a beautiful burst of blue silence, filled with layers of lit turquoise and smooth roads of sapphire. When she reaches for his hand he decides to skip the part about how being alive feels like a sword has been plunged into the place where his heart is supposed to be. By midnight the streets are empty and the night is still; a man hovers over the lock of the ice cream shop with a flashlight and a crowbar. On the pier, the mime puts the finishing touches on his new bit: "Retired Actor Opens a Restaurant." The air is thick with summer and South Beach surf ghosts. A snare drum dissolves down from the hills like a flickering flame. In the darkness, the only sounds are the cleaning of tables, the clamor of cutlery, the quiet clearing of imaginary plates.

Christy Prahl

The Grocery Pageant

We called Safeway
the food museum
and took in its exhibits weekly,
beautiful & broke,
hollowed out by plasma
& tuition,

and bored,
pooling our bills
for dry beans and rice
and all the colors they were.
The Oklahoma plains,
we fancied

> *(fluorescent lighting
> made us sentimental)*

and gazed adoringly
at the muscle we longed
to consume as the world
fell apart around us,

a teacher blowing up
on television
before reaching space,
baasskap in South Africa
& our own American
dead end streets,

bloating ourselves
ridiculous on the promise
of no worry
in our hearts or stomachs,
every chamber
filled with blood.

We pictured ourselves
grown at a long oak table,
safe in the way
of supermarkets,

whole fish & artichokes
& every manner of cake,
each shortening rosette,
curated,
like art,
like territory.

Kara Lewis

The Definition of Fermentation

Breathing without oxygen.
The catch in my mother's chest
is ripped evergreen wrapping

on Christmas morning. Tears bubble
down her cheeks like yeast when she uncovers
a breadmaker. My sister and I wait

for something to rise
like children peering into an oven, still
mesmerized by convection. Or children afraid

to reach into flame. I've watched
my mother wash the stove wishing
for sparkle. She would return

this appliance for a cellophane bracelet
flimsy and twisted by my father's fingers
or for satin glinting against her skin.

The metal box of the breadmaker is a slice
of a past life—my parents' tiny apartment, back
when my mother ate gluten. In those days, cinnamon wafted.

The hand-me-down sofa sprang lazily
when they woke. In those days, the sun spread like butter:
 pale yellow in every curtainless window.

But yeast does not require sunlight
to multiply. My sister and I are the daughter cells—matured
and prepared

for division. We know one root of bread
is *broken*, how someone has to win it and bring it
home. Another is *morsel*, as in *every last one*.

The night before she leavens
my mother arranges challah into a braid
begging my father to touch her hair.

Grace Bauer

When She Was Only Anna

She's wearing pants we might call *cropped*
or *capris*, but back then were probably
just *knickers*, an over-sized sweater,
a boy's cap perched backwards on her
straight dark hair and a pair of Mary Janes
with two-inch heels—so incongruous
for the put-up-your-dukes pose she's struck:
her left fist raised to protect her face, the right
cocked back for a punch to the gut
she looks ready to deliver. Her opponent
is dapper in his dark suit and white shirt,
his bow tie and shined dress shoes.
They appear to be on a dirt road
somewhere, spindly trees in the background,
a barely visible telephone pole.
Joe and Anna penciled on the back of the photo.

The context of the album suggests
this is all a game, elaborate posing
for a camera one of them might recently
have bought. In another shot, great aunt Sophie
wears the same cap, standing pigeon-toed
and looking impish, performing innocence
while a cocked eyebrow clearly hints
at mischief on her mind. In another,
the three of them drape themselves against
Uncle Addie's Ford like a bunch of swells.

Maybe this is how they entertained themselves,
made the kind of *good clean fun* they said

we were incapable of having when we were
the age they are here—teenagers, though I've read
that concept did not exist at the time, and soon
to be married and parents.

Joe would be dead at forty-two—*stricken*,
as the headline in the Morning Call
put it, with a heart attack in the steel mill
parking lot. His passing undoubtedly killed
whatever remnant of the defiant girl might
still have existed in her after the death of a first born
and four more kids she was left to raise alone.
Bitterness is what I mostly remember, a meanness
she doled out to her family like daily gruel,
a steady diet that evoked a like response
in the rest of us, conjuring anger
like the witch I sometimes accused her
of being, while I perfected the role
of the slut she, more than once, said I was.

The woman I knew is impossible to reconcile
with the girl in this photo—caught here
in the act of acting out some fantasy, sparring
with the man I suppose was the love of her life.
When her heart finally quit, she was just sixty-two,
but had been old for as long as I could recall.

And now I am older than she ever got to be.

Camille Hernandez

aunty culture, part 3

1.
we write memoirs in food scraps left behind
"Aunty, can you open the crab for me?" she asks
digging my thumb into its armor I free vulnerabilities
and form them into pyramids, each an artifact or mystery

2.
there are no forks on the table
a machete rests near the doorway
tired from a long day of nursing

3.
the word is magkamay, to eat with bare hands
I cannot loose fingertips of conquest from
my muscle buttons, silence is a blanket tucking
our lingering curiosities goodnight

4.
"making hamay" is to accept all the ways we crack

5.
in another country, my uncle is stirring ice cold grits
as aunty inhales the ways I play with her twang in
the gaps between my fingers. I've been told that
I am sharp but that is a synonym for impatient
to wield an inheritance of bladed wisdoms

6.
there is no word for breathing between generations.
my name is not Atlas, my shoulders bare no
punishment. Come mourning light, I'll tie

my nightgown at the knee to fertilize
the sky then gaze at the soil

7.
I am insecure about my body being
two countries tall and an ocean wide
my hipbones hold tallies of generations
surviving. My salambao is bellybutton
tall, brown as a promise and casting
nets into an unmarked constellation
of claws protecting each other

Ellen Wright

Where Old Easter Lilies Go to Die

Not to the front gate
where the meadow lilies
cluster to honk
their brassy bells at cars

Not to the edge of the drive
with the parti-colored
blooms lined up
to scrutinize arriving visitors

Not among the monastery guests
relaxing in their lawn chairs
and entertaining
the scarlet bee balm's penchant
for sticking its mohawk spikes
into their meditations

Not even to the cloister
to flatten themselves
against the silent walls
where the purple lupine effaces
its bohemian ruffles
in the shadows

But behind the tool shed
where the brothers dump them
Pentecost after Pentecost
onto the rock pile
to fend for themselves

a ragged troop
of orphaned ghost-flowers
thrust into a *danse macabre*
of desiccated iris
(that someone should have
deadheaded already)

left to veil
the bald side of the hill
in tatters of paschal finery.

Nonfiction

Tiffany Calvert

Artist's Statement, #416

My practice connects painting's history to our current visual culture, which is shaped in often confusing ways by algorithms, Artificial Intelligence, and blurred boundaries between real and virtual. I use image generating machine learning models (StyleGANs) trained on Dutch and Flemish still life paintings to create new, invented images that I print onto canvas. Using stencils to protect parts of the printed images, I paint directly onto them. These masks create hard edges where thickly applied paint meets digital reproduction.

The machine learning models, also called neural networks, produce images that are reminiscent of still life but are distorted in unexpected ways. Such unplanned variations of form can generate value. It was, in fact, a viral mutation that created the highly prized variegated patterns in the tulips depicted in the Dutch and Flemish paintings I use to train the AI—a virus that tulip growers now use AI-enabled agricultural robots to identify and eradicate.

Like AI itself the images are seductive, but the initial beauty of the paintings is a ruse. In *#416*, flowers are layered over top of one another on the canvas, some resembling the cream and crimson streaked Semper Augustus tulip, worth a fortune at the height of seventeenth century Dutch Tulip Mania. The AI generated blooms erupt with otherworldly, rogue tendrils—reproduction and painterly abstraction merge, and the attractive colors and luscious forms unfold to reveal their mutations.

The tulips depicted in historical paintings, like the non-fungible tokens used today to represent art, were exchanged as currency and were particularly ripe for economic manipulation. By recalling flower paintings, I elicit their role as aesthetic emblems of value speculation, futures trading, and Dutch colonial trade and power. In turn, my work explores the ways that painterly transgression and invention are often complicit in the expansion of speculative capitalism. Like the invisible hand of the market, AI in our lives is largely invisible. By collaborating with AI, I investigate how these neural networks shape our decisions by predicting and replicating our needs and desires.

Cover image, back cover detail: *#416*, oil on water based latex print on canvas, 22 x 28 inches, 2023. Photo by Mindy Best.

Julie Marie Wade

Four Altars

Studio

"There is an alchemy in sorrow; it can be transmuted into wisdom."
—Pearl Buck

My friend Maureen is dying, I wrote last week. Today I write, *My friend Maureen has died,* and I feel angry-grateful for this grammar: change a tense, end a life. What a strange and frightening power to hold: how the verb helps me name a loss, and how the verb seals that loss simultaneously. Grammar is the secular *amen.*

To say she has died is to kill her with language, which was of course her chosen medium. I check Wikipedia for the tenth time today. Still says *is.* "Maureen Seaton is an American LGBTQ poet, activist, and professor…" Someday I will check again, and the *is* will have become a *was.* Transmuted, right before my eyes. The *is*, I know, is already *was,* but I've hunkered down in present tense to stay. I want to live inside that *is* like the hole a woodpecker carves in a tree, disappearing so deep inside that his crest of red vanishes completely.

I have witnessed the woodpecker's vanishing in a park I love, just two miles from home. The hide-and-seek he plays while I watch him, dipping in and popping out like a magic trick.

I have witnessed Maureen's vanishing at a distance of two thousand miles, in the room I've seen on Zoom, the bed I've seen on Zoom—home hospice care—her daughter standing close and holding up the phone, setting up the screen, Maureen reading poems that ping across the miles. I marvel that Maureen's hair is as red, even in death, as the woodpecker's pileated crown.

Before hospice, before the "medical leave" that transmuted into retirement, before cancer, before the inconclusive screening that became cancer, conclusively, in a callback voice message, Maureen lived in a studio apartment on Hayes Street, just east of North Ocean Drive—

sometimes with her partner, always with her dog—fifty feet or so from the Hollywood Broadwalk. Everyone thinks we misspell it or mistype it, but it's not a *boardwalk*. Does that even matter now? Nothing wooden here. It's *broad*, lots of room for strolling and milling and renting surreys and eating ice cream that melts faster than we can slurp it down.

I run on this Broadwalk at sunrise most days. I run past Hayes Street and wave to Maureen's apartment—as if she still lives there. I have always done this, as if she might step outside with her little dog and her huge sunglasses and wave back at me, then walk toward me and the sea. Once upon a time, she did. And then she didn't live there anymore, but she lived somewhere—she was *living*, the active verb—and I missed her in Kendall, and I missed her in Colorado, but she was living all the while. I loved that she was living, and when I learned that she was going to die sooner rather than later, I cherished the fact of her living harder. I waved longer and circled back to the apartment on Hayes Street. I don't know who lives there now. I don't know if I want to know.

But I return at sunrise most days, as I did the morning after I learned she had left this world. Like a penitent before an altar? No. More like an acolyte remembering the way I once lit candles in my Lutheran church. Not running then, walking, with a slow, solemn gait toward the altar, where I would bow and then recede through a silent side door. Maureen was a candle I did not light—she was already glowing when I met her. Now I bow before her old apartment and think of the flame that was her hair. What did Eliot say? I call him back: *objective correlative*. The flaming hair that was the fire of life she carried. *Unsnuffable*, I thought then. Now, the bow becomes a kind of keeling.

Garbo Grabber

> "I will try not to rage
> as palms uproot and the wind blows me into something
> sharp and concrete."
> —Denise Duhamel

Here in South Florida, I live inside a postcard. Our beaches are exactly as advertised on the 4 x 6 cardstock photos sold at Publix and Walgreens and even in our smallest gas stations, our fly-by-night mini-marts. Just spin the racks, and you'll see miles of golden sand, cerulean waves breaking in white spume along the shore, brown pelicans and blue herons diving. "Yes, it really looks like that, *exactly* like that," I confirm to every friend who contemplates a visit.

In eleven years, it's not that I've ever grown inured to this beauty. It's more that I've begun to brace for this beauty's demise. All the credible experts say we're living on borrowed time—all of us, true, but especially those of us who make our homes this close to the southeastern coast. The ocean is rising, the coral reefs are dying, and the hurricanes grow stronger every year. I try to listen to the music of the tides, but predictions overwhelm me with their ominous noise: *We've got maybe twenty years left before the sea reclaims this place, before coastal Florida becomes completely uninhabitable.*

This summer, like every summer since we moved here, my in-laws came from Louisville for a visit. They rented a house on Hollywood Beach just a mile from where we live in Dania. One evening we were sitting in the living room, swimsuits dangling on the drying rack, pizzas baking in the oven, and all at once, the sky switched from blue to black. No warning: it was day, then suddenly, prematurely, night. The lightning and thunder nearly simultaneous. We watched purple ribbons scissor the air, heard a din like all the plates crashing down from their cosmic shelves. Awe one moment, fear the next. This is the way of storms here. Within minutes, the side road leading to the beach had flooded. My nephew shouted, "Look! The street has waves in it!" Palm fronds caught in the sluice clotted the visible sewage drains. Water backing up, water pouring down, and across the vacant parking lot, we saw how the stairs leading to Ocean's 13 Bar & Grill transformed into a treacherous waterfall.

Then, just as swiftly as it began, the storm was over. The sky lightened to lavender, and the marshy patches of weed and grass glistened silver in the aftermath. *Beautiful danger*, I murmured, as if this were a new thought and not my most persistent revelation. Strangest to me is the way a certain amnesia proceeds from our held breath, our clutched phones glowing with The Weather Channel's latest update. When a storm passes, we forget the threat, dismiss the foreshadowing as *sui generis*. My niblings scampered away from the windows. The pizzas summoned us to the dinner table. But later, when I peered out at the road again, I saw how the wind had thrown over the bins—the huge blue one labeled Landfill, the huge green one labeled Recycling. They floated on their sides, lids gaping wide and waste eddying everywhere.

"Where are you going?" my wife asked as I laced up my shoes. I pointed to the shiny black garbage bags and the smaller white ones—for kitchen and bathroom trash—many of which had ripped open. Sodden Pampers, fast food wrappers, assorted plastics, aluminum cans. "It's a wasteland out there," I replied—"*literally*."

Knowing how much I long to help, to *do something* to prevent—or at least delay—our community's ongoing decay, Angie had bought me a "garbo grabber" for my birthday. The feel-good company that sells it, based in Palm Beach, has a Save Our Oceans motto, and all purchases are meant to benefit South Florida eco-conservation projects. "Instead of one of those old men who wanders around with a metal detector at sunrise," she said, "you can take your grabber and pick up whatever doesn't belong." *But who's to say it won't all end up back in the ocean?* That's the question that lurks in italics under every approving nod, every cheer of support from strangers and friends.

That evening I walked out into lavender light, solitary and cringing as dirty water filled my shoes. *Don't think about it!* the hardest commandment of my life, yet there I was, trying to adhere. I righted the bins with solemn attention, the way I once stood before the pastor in my church thirty years before, waiting to be confirmed. Sometimes the ritual of Confirmation was called "affirmation of baptism." When we were infants and far too young to recall, our parents held us near the altar as the pastor doused our heads with water. Twelve or thirteen years later, we were expected to return to that place, to *choose* for ourselves the holy path that first water symbolized. I remember returning, but not avowing, a single word the pastor said.

In the window, my niblings held up Scattergories, Scrabble, other games they knew I liked to play. They banged on the glass and shouted for me to come inside, but I had chosen something else, futile perhaps, and I was trying not to think about it. Grab by grab, I lifted filthy refuse from the road. As counterpoint to stench, I tried to conjure the smells I love the most: bonfires on the beach, coconut-infused sunscreen, fresh lemons squeezed into water or cola. It didn't work. Maybe ten minutes passed, maybe twenty, maybe longer. *How did we produce so much waste?* I moved slowly but deliberately. Sometimes I held my breath, and sometimes I gagged. When I finished, I dragged the heavy bins up the long drive, wedged them in a small bed of rocks. Weary, sullied, but oddly elated, too, I left my prayer at the altar of Missouri Street and North Ocean Drive: *Make it matter, God—whatever you are. Let my small gesture be of some consequence after all.*

Postcards

"—One day it happens: what you have feared all your life, the unendurably specific, the exact thing. No matter what you say or do."
—Marie Howe

Mornings during quarantine, I wrote postcards to my friend's mother in Rhode Island. I had met Jan many times when she was still strong enough to travel to South Florida, but just before the pandemic began, she fell—a hard fall, her worst fall yet—and was forced to move into Mount Saint Rita. This was the same facility where she had once worked as a nurse, where her own mother had passed away decades before, and where she had always feared her own life would end.

I wrote to Jan because she was lonely and unable to receive visitors. I wrote to Jan because I liked sending words out into the world to someone who would be happy to receive them. I wrote to Jan because I could not bring myself to write to my own mother.

It was a peaceful ritual: coming to my desk at first light, gazing out at the frangipani tree, which always effervesced with blossoms. No down time for that tree, no fallow season. Squirrels would nibble from the clusters of orange berries, and the hot pink blooms would drop to the lawn one by one, bodacious as '80s spandex between the spiky blades of green.

"Two iguanas live in our neighborhood," I wrote. "The smaller one we call Simon—he's bright as a shamrock with black rings around his tail—and the larger one we call Garfunkel—he's orange as a traffic cone. Together they patrol the cul-de-sac, trusting the cats and ducks will make way for them, which of course they do. These iguanas have moxie."

I described a snake gliding along the garden wall, a cardinal building her nest in the cypress tree, a dormant orchid suddenly burgeoning again in dainty splendor. Images of hope, I hoped. Descriptions, not reflections. These images freed me from needing to speak of fear or pain, all the uncertainties that attended our lives.

After a year at Mount Saint Rita, Jan was moved into hospice care and died the summer visitors were allowed to return. My friend was there with her mother during her final hours, as the priest administered last rites and a family blessing. The bare room became the altar. When Jan died, I sat at my desk with a stack of postcards, silent, bereft—all that white space glaring back at me. I stared at my uncapped pen, my roll of stamps on the windowsill, unsure of what to do next.

I still didn't write to my mother.

This week I crossed another threshold in my life, another birthday. I have always welcomed each new age with joy, adding numbers to my life like marbles or seashells in a treasured collection. Now we can be with others again, sharing space and meals, squeezing together for a picture. I went out with my friends for tacos at the beach, body-surfing in the ocean. I didn't think about the way my life began, only about the way my life was going. *Being present,* I congratulated myself.

Then, a card arrived from my mother, and the sight of her tight, precise script on the envelope filled me with dread. *What was my mother doing at forty-four, the age I am now?* Visiting her best friend in the hospital, refusing to take me with her once Joanne had lost her hair. She didn't want me to remember Joanne that way. "Blue and bloated," she described her. And then Joanne died. I remember my mother dressed in black for the funeral mass, wearing a hat with a little veil that hid the tears in her eyes. She dropped me at school, refused to write a note, to let me follow her into that church or anywhere close to her grief.

My wife opens the card at my request. I pace around the house, busy myself with chores, but I can feel her reading in the next room, and the dread deepens. "Highlights?" I ask, and she shakes her head. "It wasn't a good one." There has never been a good one. "This card is more of an…ultimatum." The frangipani tree billows in the background. The squirrels chatter as they chase each other along its narrow branches. "An ultimatum?" Angie nods. "She says that she's waited as long as she's going to wait for you to come to your senses. So if you don't come home now—and she stresses the point *alone*—then she and your father will cut you out of their will for good." It honestly hadn't occurred to me that they hadn't done so already. "So this is just a threat, a threat of disinheritance?" Angie slides the card back inside its envelope. I note the jagged edge. "You don't need to read this," she says softly. "There is no kindness here." My head, swirling. "But—does she really believe—after all these years—the way to lure me back into her life is with *money*? Not love, not acceptance of who I am, who *you* are, but money?" Hot pink petals, outside the window, falling. "I'm afraid so."

Today I sit at my desk, the blank postcard before me, the uncapped pen, the festive stamp that proclaims *Celebrate*! It's the only kind of stamp I have.

For many years, I knelt as supplicant before the altar of my mother, she who was god-like always, larger than life. Then, one day I did not kneel but told her simply about the one I loved, the life I wanted. A harsh rebuking followed, and I knew, from that day forward, that I would have to seek my sanctuary elsewhere. *Money?* It was never about money. How could it be? But it was never about sin either or needing to atone for my heart's true tide.

I try to write about the view outside my window, the iguanas lumbering along the street, the zenaida doves, newly alighted, grooming each other's wings. Description, not reflection, remember? But this is it, the unendurably specific thing. I consider *good-bye*. I consider *amen*. Finally, I address the postcard—*Mother, Your House on the Hill*—then drop it in the mail uninscribed.

Fire

"We built altars everywhere and never went back."
—Maureen Seaton

There are stories we keep writing, keep telling ourselves our whole lives, wondering if we will finally learn the lessons they were meant to teach.

Once in graduate school, more than twenty years ago now, I wrote in a poem: "Altars are for alterations./ I could never be cut from the same cloth/ as my parents." I felt proud of my word play, the little jab I could take at marriage, that new eluder, that thing I believed I would never have.

My friend says our lives are more like poems than stories anyway: recursive, enjambed, with at least one major volta before they close. My volta came when I was still so young, just twenty-two, all broken lines and *via negativa* style. I did not put on the dress, though I did find it beautiful, especially the bodice woven with flowers—each pistil a pearl—and the way it could be lifted off, worn separately from the wide, white skirt. I did not travel down Interstate 5 to the orchard three hours away, did not meet my would-be groom under an apple tree, where he and his brother, also our priest, were waiting. I did not call. I did not write. Instead, I went to the movies with the woman I loved and lost myself in two hours of screen time.

The movie, it sounds apocryphal now, was *Little Altars Everywhere*.

What a strange thing, a poignant thing, to give up marriage for love when all my life I had been taught to link them—that old tandem bicycle from the theme park song. But then my life-is-a-poem friend suggested how much better to love without marriage than to marry without love, and that sustained me, sustained us, Angie and me, for years and years.

Of course there was still the matter of the unworn wedding dress, wrapped in its pink garment bag—how it traveled with us year after year, home after home, toppling from each Uhaul like a mammoth cupcake, billowing from the backs of closets, a little white fringe caught in each door. Angie said we could make curtains, but neither of us knew how. It didn't feel right to give it away—my satin volta, my frocked end-stop—yet it loomed larger as time passed, casting a broader shadow. The sight of pink sheen and white pleats, in the closet no less, came to remind me of the fiancé I left, the harm I caused. I wanted it to become something else—to *morph*.

We made our own ritual then, with friends we had made along the way. One had a barrel in her backyard for burning things. Another, a photographer, brought black cat firecrackers to start the fire and her camera to capture the scene. A third friend brought carburetor fluid, which he said would "accelerate the blaze."

I had just written a book called *Small Fires*. The title's meaning was partly literal, partly metaphorical. As a child, after my mother found and read my journal, she insisted that I burn the offending portions, page by page—places where I mentioned her, unfavorably, where I complained about her rage and need to control. How I longed for a roomier existence, freedom to choose for myself what I wanted, even if it was only the shirt I wore or the song I listened to on the way home from school. These are, after all, the small details that make up a life, and I was desperate even at twelve, thirteen, to forge my own. My mother struck the first match and handed it to me. Later, I burned the rest and kept the ashes in a jar.

Those first pages I burned against my will, but the dress I burned by choice, a choice Angie and I had made together. The orange flames roiled, and the dress seemed to take flight like that burning bird of myth. Not a *small* fire at all—it morphed to inferno as we watched, mesmerized, two extinguishers standing by in the bright dusk, and all the while, Sara taking pictures.

Not long after the dress went up in smoke, new laws of marriage equality began to proliferate. I thought of Adrienne Rich, "the thing itself and not the myth." Maybe the dress was the myth of marriage, and suddenly, severed from the old story, a poem could rise in its place. Soon, we flew across the country. We dressed in black. We exchanged vows in a bar on a Monday night, in the middle of winter, as snow fleeced the ground. Nothing *by the book* and everything by the heart. We leaned in, we spoke up, so even the strangers in the main dining room could hear. Love had altered us after all, and an altar might anywhere appear.

Maybe it was that night, or the next one, when I said to Angie, "Remember how we went to see *Little Altars Everywhere* the first time I was supposed to get married?" It had been almost thirteen years. She shook her head and tucked her cold hand inside my pocket. "That was *The Divine Secrets of the Ya-Ya Sisterhood*," she said. I squinted, disbelieving. "Are you sure?" She nodded, and I watched the snowflakes glistening in her hair. "*Little Altars Everywhere* was the prequel."

Fiction

Gregory Byrd

Boy Abducted by Bear

"It looked like a big dog carrying something along," the man said. He was on top of his barn outside Ocala when he saw it move across a field and lope towards woods. That was the first report. Then, a woman driving home from visiting her mother saw a big man sitting on a log next to a child and when she asked if they could use a ride, the man turned into a bear that ran off into a swampy area where there were cedars. She was so shaken she couldn't recall if the bear had the child by the hand or if it was carrying the boy. Only two days ago a worker coming out to check on the blueberry plants near Ocala came upon the bear and the boy sitting on the ground eating something. The worker, a Spaniard from Tampa, ran off towards the main building screaming, "Bear! Bear! Bring the gun!" but by the time he came back with the manager and the gun, the bear and the boy were gone, and she admitted they were a good fifty or sixty paces away. A tracker found bear scat with berries and fish bones in it. And human scat with the same. A rose-colored button was found at the scene.

    When they called at the house, I'd hoped they were calling for a job spotting game or even that big carnival I had contacted about giving airplane rides, but it was the game warden from Ocala saying it wasn't strictly a matter for the sheriff and he was afraid the good 'ol boys from up there would hurt the child if they went after the bear so he was using them as a last resort and hoping I'd be able to spot the bear and the boy from the air. The fifty dollars he was offering wasn't much considering my time and fuel for the Jenny, but it was better than sitting at home in Dunedin waiting for something to happen, so I drove over to the airfield and checked out the engine, cleaned the plugs, bought thirty gallons of gasoline, and put twenty of it in the main tank and another ten in the upper wing tank.

    I'd flown up the coast towards Cedar Key before and once flew a businessman up to Jacksonville so he didn't have to take the train. Maybe

Ocala was 120 miles. That would put me at an hour and a half-two hours, depending on wind and how close to top speed the Jenny would fly. She was stable but, heavens was she slow. Even the earlier Sopwiths, the Pups, I flew in France would do close to a hundred but if the Jenny was doing seventy-five, she was running full-out. Of course, the French SPAD biplanes and English SEs were doing 120-130 before the war was over and Billy Mitchell flew somewhere over 220 in his Curtiss last year, but such machines required money or flying for the military—two things I either didn't have or didn't want anymore. In the Jenny, you had no choice but to take things easy, watch the red shouldered hawks that would sport with you, see the sharks patrolling off the beach or the dolphins in their pods which chased the sharks away, or flocks of birds that rose up off lakes as you flew over. You scanned the skies for other airplanes when you were near a city, but usually you didn't see much away from there and it was more important in this sort of flying to watch for storms and be sure there was a place to set down.

I spread the Rand McNally Atlas open on the lower wing and weighted it with the rifle and the thermos. Those days, we used road maps just as well as anything, and while I could follow a railroad, on the map, I traced a route up the coast from Dunedin to Anclote Keys, Weekiwatchee River, Chassahowitzka and Homosassa Rivers, Crystal Bay to the Withlachoochee River just south of Yankeetown. This was where I'd make my turn east and follow the Withlacoochee and head east-northeast towards Ocala. It was good to have landmarks that were hard to miss. In 1917, we had a German two-seater land at our aerodrome in Saint-Pol-sur-Mer because the coast could look the same in bad light all the way up through Belgium. My mechanic, Bernard, met the machine with his automatic pistol and a squad of Tommies. Even in bad visibility and haze that evening, he knew the engine didn't sound like one of ours. If I somehow missed the Withlacoochee, the coast turned directly west at Waccasassee Bay and I could just turn due east towards Ocala. Straight north would take me over Rosewood in no time. Cedar Key was west.

Of course, it would be hard to identify anything in Rosewood now. Maybe the general store, if I recalled right, but the burned houses would be obvious compared to those still standing in Wylly or Sumner.

In early January, I hadn't yet heard that they'd burned the negro town there yet, but when I stopped by Eddie's house in Dunedin then, he had a Springfield rifle when he answered the door.

"Hunting hogs today, Eddie? I came to ask about laying those bricks at Mom's house."

"Nosir, Mr. Russell. Not hogs but men if they come by."

"And why would they come by?" He rested the Springfield in the corner behind the door and shut the door behind me.

"You didn't hear about Rosewood yet?"

"Eddie, I haven't seen a newspaper nor a soul in five days. I flew the Jenny down south and just stayed down near the Everglades and fished."

"They killed all the negroes or drove them off up there. Then went back and burned them out after one man shot two of the white folks coming for him."

I sighed and looked him in the eyes. "Well, shit," I said.

"Yessuh. Shit for sure."

"Klan's busy up around there, I think. Gainesville, anyway."

"They's here, too, Mr. Rusty."

"I know."

"When I came back from France, they come by the house and were waiting out front. I loaded the rifle and was trying to figure out what to do next when I see the sheriff come by and talk to them. 'Well, Bobby,' the one tells the sheriff, 'We come to tell this colored boy not to get uppity just because he wore a uniform in France and killed some Germans. We ain't having him struttin' around.' The sheriff leaned on his holstered pistol and said, 'Boys, don't you know Eddie? He's a good negro. And he wasn't in that fighting, anyway, like that Harlem unit. He dug ditches and drove trucks. Y'all need to get your story straight because I ain't putting up with y'all making trouble around here. Now git on home.'"

"They dispersed off my front step," Eddie continued, "and the sheriff came to my front door. 'How you doing, Mr. Johnson?' he said. I said I was fine, and he said, 'Those boys thought you were someone to cause trouble since you come back from the Army, but you're not a troublemaker, are you?' I said nawsir, I wasn't. 'And you don't have a firearm or anything, do you?' I said nawsir, but I knew he could see my rifle over in the corner. But I tell you, Mr. Russell, I killed me two men in France—one I shot in the chest with this here rifle and one with a bayonet through his throat and I didn't like it not one bit."

"*All a bloody balls*, as my major over there would have called it."

"Yasir, that's what it seems like."

There was a sound in the kitchen and Eddie called, "It's okay. You can come out." A negro girl of maybe fifteen came out of the kitchen. She looked to Eddie and then to me and back to him.

"Mr. Russell is my friend. I've known his family many years. Say hello." I reached out my hand and the girl stretched it out as far from her body as she could. Her hand was trembling when I shook it.

"Sally is my . . . cousin. Visiting from . . . up north near Tallahassee," Eddie said.

"Good to meet you, Sally," I said. She retreated into the kitchen.

"I can come by and look at that brick job tomorrow, Mr. Russell."

"That'll do fine. Mom's been on me about it since Christmas."

That was maybe a month ago and I never saw Sally since then. It was clear that there was something Eddie wouldn't share even with me about the whole situation but now, getting ready to fly north towards Rosewood, I thought about all of that again. They said the negroes from Rosewood had scattered into the swamps and some had boarded a train going north. I wondered if some had come south, too, stayed with friends or relatives. But my issue was not with the negroes from Rosewood, but with the bear.

In the passenger compartment of the Jenny, I lashed down the Lee-Enfield I'd brought back from France. It wasn't easy to find cartridges for it in the United States, but the Tommies guarding our airfield had taught me to shoot it and they were so cheap after the war that it made sense somehow to bring one home on the boat. I didn't relish the idea of shooting the bear, but it seemed that someone was going to shoot it eventually and there was the boy to worry about, too.

I kept the steel Stanley thermos with coffee in the cockpit with me and a sandwich made with ham, and a bottle with a stopper in case I needed to pee and couldn't find a place to set down. I kept the binoculars with me, too, though it was hard to use them from the air while you were flying. I stashed the whiskey with my change of clothes and oilcloth lashed to the front seat. It was February so most of the afternoon rainstorms hadn't started. That was good because you could spend all afternoon trying to navigate around one of those storms and sometimes you found that it wasn't a storm but a whole line of storms and you kept trying to fly east or west to get around it until you found there was no going around it and you flew into it if you had no choice or found a place to set down and then sheltered under a wing until it got past. But it would be good flying weather for another couple of months in Florida. Some of the pilots down here wouldn't fly when it was cold, but they didn't know cold like we knew it in France—twenty below at a fifteen thousand.

Where were the boys who hung around the field looking for free rides that day when I need a prop pull? At school, probably. What was it that day, nine o'clock on a Tuesday? I reached in and made sure the switch was off, then swung the prop through twice, then back to the cockpit to turn the switch on. Swung once and it spit and coughed. Then, on the second swing, she caught and the engine roared. I ducked around the prop and wing and pulled the chocks and up into the cockpit before she started moving forward without me.

The sock showed a light quartering breeze. No one else was flying that day, so I taxied out onto the grass strip and pulled on my helmet and goggles. Someone outside a hangar working on a two-seater waved at me as I firewalled the throttle and the Jenny pulled down the runway, then the tail was up and she lifted herself into the air. She doesn't jump up like the Pup, almost immediately, but she's running on the ground and then she's flying and it's hard to know where one thing ends and the other begins. Climbed out to the south, then banked west towards the coastline. There was the Fort Harrison Hotel. I turned north from Clearwater and flew down St. Joseph Sound. There was what was once Hog Island that's now cut in two and there was the new Fenway Hotel in Dunedin. Eight hundred feet. We climbed. Another five minutes we might make two thousand feet. She'd top out at maybe six thousand. Crazy. Climbing over the Somme, we'd end up at fifteen thousand or eighteen thousand feet where you could see the curve of the earth and the sky was a particular blue and your face would freeze. No—nothing was warlike about the Jenny. I might push her to seventy miles per hour but that was about it. Like sailing, no matter how much of a hurry you were in, she would take her own time. She wasn't twitchy, but she kept your feet busy on the rudder bar.

A thousand feet, passing Sutherland. I opened the flipboard with the map on it, but there wasn't any real need. I could follow the coast and then turn west with the Withlacoochee. I'd flown this route before, sometimes to deliver mail or medicine to Cedar Key. On the way back once, I put two bushels of oysters in the front seat for the Fenway and sold them for twelve dollars they were so fresh. It would make the most sense to follow the railroad up, but I loved the coastline and the water.

After stopping in Crystal River for fuel and calling the Ocala sheriff, it was close to two o'clock by the time I approached Ocala. I'd turned east around Yankeetown and picked up the C.L. railroad and followed it northeast towards Ocala, and it was around York where I saw the blueberry fields and, at the southern edge, saw the police cars parked there and could see the men and the dogs fanning out across the fields—sheriff had called them out, apparently. They waved and I wagged the wings. The fields ran maybe two miles in either direction so the bear could be hiding anywhere along them or in the woods surrounding the fields. From the air, I should be able to see the bear when it ran between the rows of bushes.

I flew east, out towards the edge of Ocala, then flew back west over the fields, starting at the southern edge at about eight hundred feet. High enough to not spook the bear, I hoped, but close enough to see him. The men with the guns and dogs were spread out maybe twenty yards apart and I guessed that some of them were deputies and some of them were hunters from the area hoping to kill the bear. Even from up high, I could see the dogs straining at their leashes. When I called him in Crystal River, the sheriff said they'd found a sleeve from a boy's shirt, and I imagined they were scenting the dogs with that. On the first pass, all I saw was the hunting—I mean rescue—party. Near York, I turned and flew east again.

I was probably a mile into the search pattern when I saw the boy and the bear. They were both running north, over the rows of plants, which was strange, because instead of running towards the woods, they ran towards the railroad. I chopped power to about forty miles per hour, just above stalling and watched them running. The boy was a negro boy, something they hadn't told me. And there was something strange about the bear. It certainly looked like a bear—black coat like a bear's—but it didn't move like a bear. From the air, a bear ran like a big dog, but this one seemed to stumble along mostly on two legs, sometimes dropping to three or four. Even stranger, the boy stayed with the bear and even helped it along when it stumbled. Maybe it was an old bear and senile or something and that's why it took up with the boy.

I imagine the search party had seen me circling and would be working their way towards my position. Especially after the sheriff said that some of those boys were excited to shoot the bear, well, I didn't trust them not to shoot the boy, too. Rosewood was only a stone's throw and it was likely those boys were involved in all that craziness. If they'd burn a house and run all those colored people out, they'd shoot a negro boy to get to a bear.

An access road ran along part of the railroad to the north. It shown bright tan when I flew over it on the way in. If I could set down there, I could head off the boy and the bear before the search party made it to us. I powered up and climbed back to eight hundred feet and found the railroad again and then flew over the road looking for electrical and telephone wires. Some places had electrical wires now and you had to be careful or you'd tangle up on landing and wreck your kite. As I thought, further east, there were telegraph wires across the road. You could see them if you knew what you were looking for. A little further west, closer to the field, the road seemed to be clear and a section of it passed close to the railroad, so I could run parallel to it and set down on the road if I watched the telephone poles on the other side of the tracks. I took two passes before I was comfortable setting down, and the Jenny bounced down the dirt road until she came to a stop. The wings stuck out too close to the tracks for my comfort, but I hadn't seen any trains from the air.

I pulled off my helmet and goggles, unbuckled and climbed out of the airplane. It was quiet there and always seemed so quiet after the rush of air past your ears, the noise of the engine and the big fan of the propeller up front. I untied the Lee-Enfield from the front seat and chambered a round. I walked further west, where I imagined the boy and the bear would come out eventually. The hunting dogs were baying maybe a mile away. At the very least, they would drive the bear this way, even if the bear didn't mean to head to the railroad. A few birds chirped and four ducks flew overhead, going south. My ears adjusted more to the quiet of the country. I must have waited ten minutes before I saw them.

By the time I heard the crashing sounds coming through the fields, I could hear the dogs more clearly and I could hear the voices of the men as they shouted at the dogs and at each other. The crashing of the boy and bear running through the underbrush got louder and I raised the rifle and released the safety. And then, there they were, in front of me, the boy with threadbare blue pants and a torn, red, shirt and no shoes. The bear came out of the field behind him, its black coat tattered, and the boy ran and took its hand and said, "Mama, Mama!"

The woman lifted the blanket off her and said, "Go ahead and shoot me now! You done killed my husband already, but leave my boy be!" The dogs bayed more and more loudly and I could hear one of the men yelling, "Over this way! I saw them go this way!" And the woman was crying and the boy was holding her hand when I saw a black bear come out of the field, flushed by the dogs, charging straight for where the woman and the boy stood not ten yards in front of me. As I raised the rifle and aimed it, the woman covered her face and ducked down to cover the boy.

"Oh, Jesus!" she cried, and I fired just to her left. The first bullet caught the bear on the shoulder and he howled. But the .303 round wasn't enough there to stop him, or his running from the dogs filled him with so much adrenaline that he wasn't ready to lie down yet. I chambered another round and fired again as he stood up. There were shouts from in the field as they heard my shots. I loaded and fired again and the bear dropped, black bear blood pouring into the Florida sand.

The woman cried hysterically, and I shook her. "I'm not gonna hurt you, but those that are coming might! Listen to me!" She looked into my eyes and somehow drew quiet as she quivered. "You go over to the other side of the railroad tracks. There's a field maybe a half mile north. I'll pick you up there, you hear? I promise I'll take care of your boy. Hurry, they're coming!"

I don't know why she trusted me, but she moved as fast as she could over the tracks. I pulled some smoked mullet from the Jenny, gave some to the boy and tossed some around. I rubbed the boy's shirt over the bear to confuse the scents and then put it back on him.

"Listen, son. Listen to me." The boy sniffled and looked into my eyes with terror. "I'm gonna help you and your ma, but you gotta do what I say, okay?" The boy nodded his head. "You were on your way to Gainesville to see your grandmother and you got lost. That bear took you in, okay? You just tell them that and I'll get you and your ma someplace safe." He nodded again.

I was standing above the bear with my rifle when the first two men with dogs came out of the field. One had a shotgun raised and the other had what looked like a lever action 30-30.

"What the hell'd you shoot him with?" the first man said.

"Lee-Enfield. .303."

".303? Never heard of that around here."

"It's an English rifle. Brought it back from France."

"Oh, that's where you flew. Well, Charlie's going to be disappointed he didn't get it."

The boy stood there, looking at the bear.

"No one told us it was a black boy, but makes sense he'd take up with a *black* bear!" The other men who had come laughed loudly and one took a pull from a flask. "What you doin' out here, boy?"

The boy shivered and moved behind my leg.

"Ease up on him. I just shot his friend and he's been wandering in the woods with a bear for a week." I stared the man in the eye.

The sheriff had caught up with everyone by this point. "Ease up on the boy, Jeb. He ain't old enough to cause anyone trouble. Now, what are you doing out here in the woods with this bear, boy?" The boy looked up at me.

"It's okay, you can tell him. He's a sheriff."

"I'm . . . I'm going to see my grandmama in Gainesville and got off the train for a minute when it stopped and then I got lost when it went on without me, suh."

"That's why you ain't to get off the train, boy."

"Yessuh, but I had use the terlet and man said I couldn't use the one in the train car."

The dogs were sniffing around confusedly, eating bits of smoked mullet and sniffing at the bear. I set the boy on the wing of the Jenny. Somebody with the search party had a camera and commenced to taking pictures—me with the bear, me with the boy and the bear, the search party with the bear, the boy holding the bear's paw and crying. I shared some of my coffee with the boy. I convinced the sheriff it would be easiest if I just flew the boy up to Gainesville to his grandmother's house and have him out of everyone's way. The search party was happy to get the Jenny turned around so I could take off. It was just in time, too, because I could hear a train rumbling from a ways off. I swung the prop and jumped in the cockpit and firewalled the engine. It was tight with the wings so close to the tracks on one side and trees and brush on the other but we pulled up before the telegraph wires on the east end of the road. We flew over the train as it rumbled along westwards.

"We're up in the air like a bird, mister?" the boy shouted from the front seat.

"Yes, we are!"

"Are we gonna fall?"

"Not if I can help it!"

The boy's mother was in the field where I had told her to go, but it took some coaxing to get her in the plane.

"We gonna fly like birds, Mama!" her son told her.

It turned out they really did have family near Gainesville, and I dropped them in Fairbanks, where they helped me find a service station and fuel up the Jenny. The woman's aunt and uncle brought us into their house and made us coffee and gave us dinner. After what had happened in Rosewood, I wasn't surprised they kept looking at me so strangely.

"You ain't from around here," the uncle said.

"Clearwater. My people come from French Canada. Quebec."

"You heard what they did in Rosewood."

"Yeah. I did." What could I say that wasn't obvious? I started to think about the incident in France, where the German soldiers were killing a French squad and I flew over the area too late to save them. How I wasn't there when my father died. I would tell them how the Klan had burned my grandmother's French Canadian church in Maine but they probably wouldn't believe me. "Terrible," I said. "You'd think that after the war and the flu, people would have had enough of killing."

"You mean you figure *white folks* would have had enough of killing." He held me with his eyes, accusing me.

"I imagine you're right. I saw lots of colored people in the war, too. Killing is killing and ain't none of it is much good," I said. "Didn't even like killing that bear." They didn't say it, but I knew the woman and the boy had been in Rosewood. I imagined they had tried to jump the train or had walked out and got turned around.

The days were short in February, so I slept in the front room of their house with the Lee-Enfield beside me. In the morning, I loaded the Jenny and checked my map, then took off and followed the Sea Air Line railroad down to Cedar Key. Flying in the morning made me think about flying in France and I scanned the skies for other machines without even being aware I was doing so—behind, above, far in the distance. The railroad ran right through Rosewood on my way to the coast. One house had a burned-through roof, and I could see into the interior where it had collapsed. A store or something had met pretty much the same fate.

From there, I climbed and headed south over the Gulf of Mexico. I climbed until the Jenny couldn't go any higher and I was five miles off the coast. It was safer to be where I could always land, but, at least for a little while, I didn't want to be around anyone at all.

Robert Sachs

Wary

The call from Charles was unexpected. Years ago in high school we were on the same debate team. We were friendly. Cordial may be a better word. But we weren't friends. I remember that he lived with an elderly aunt; no other family or friends. I felt sorry for him. I never saw him smile. Not once in four years of high school. A serious kid. Short and skinny; I doubt he weighed much more than a hundred pounds. Dark curly hair cut short. He was the only guy to wear a white shirt and tie to school—always the same thin black tie. Every single day. He was a pretty good student, but while he got good grades, they were never great. B, B minus kind of thing. No one called him Chuck. Or even Charlie. That would have been too informal for Charles. I lost track of him after high school, until, years later, I read in the paper he was going to prison.

The article said he had been convicted of using a sophisticated check kiting scheme that allowed him to live well beyond his meager means as an assistant manager of a woman's shoe store. "Mister Clean?" one of my friends shouted when I told him the news. "That little prick. Black tie my ass. A con artist. Shoulda known."

"He got five years. Could be out in three," I said. "Sad." At least I thought it was sad. Not many people agreed with me. One of my friends called me naive.

And then Charles called. Out of the blue. No "what have you been doing." No "I heard you got divorced." He needed a favor, is what he said. His dog, Wary, needed a place to stay.

"While you're in prison?" I asked.

"Yeah." He didn't admit or deny anything. Didn't explain. Just "Yeah."

"He's a small dog," he said. "A gray and white ball of fur. I couldn't stand it if he had to go to a shelter. You'll keep him for me?"

No small talk about the old days. No buttering me up. Just the ask. I surprised myself by saying yes.

He didn't thank me. "Great," he said. "Someone will drop him off. Take good care of him."

Two days later, a sheriff's deputy rang my doorbell. "All yours," he said, handing me a small metal cage containing Wary. He also gave me an open box of dog treats and a manila envelope. "Instructions," he said.

The sheet of instructions included things like brush him every day and bathe him once a week. There was an approved list of foods.

"You're nuts," one of my friends said. "Have you ever even had a dog?"

"This will be my first."

"Why do you think he asked you?"

"Who knows. Maybe I was nice to him once."

"That must be it," my friend said. "And why, Mr. Nice Guy, did you say yes?"

"Character defect?"

My friend nodded in agreement. "Bingo."

I read that this breed—a cross between a Havanese and a Maltese—was smart and active. Wary appeared to be neither. For the first two weeks, he would leave his cage only to eat and relieve himself, the latter on (or close to) a cloth mat I stationed six feet from the cage. If I carried him to my backyard, he'd toddle back up the three steps to the porch and lie there. He didn't bark. Ever. My attempts to engage him fell on deaf, floppy ears.

A couple of weeks later, Charles called. "The prison charges me ten cents a minute," he said. He wanted to talk briefly with Wary. After that he called every day. Between seven and seven thirty. It wasn't long before the dog began anticipating the calls. If I didn't answer the phone fast enough to suit him, Wary would growl. I'd move the phone close to his cage and turn on the speaker. Charles would say, "Wary," and the dog would get out of his cage and run around the telephone, yapping. He'd calm down while Charles told him how his day was going.

"The food here is terrible," he'd tell his dog. "It's hard for me to sleep. I share a cell with a fat man who cheated on his taxes. Snores like a son of a bitch." Things like that. Mundane things. And Wary stood there listening, his tail slowly moving back and forth. Ten minutes and then

Charles would say goodbye. Wary would return to his cage. "Talk to you tomorrow."

He never bothered to ask me how we were getting along, whether Wary was eating well, whether he was getting enough sleep and exercise. Nothing. It was as if the dog's sole role was to listen to Charles.

Wary and I did not grow close. We did not develop a loving relationship. To me, he was an interloper, a pain in the ass. To him, I was a nameless servant.

It went on like this for almost a year and then the calls from Charles stopped. Wary was confused. He looked suspiciously at me as if I was somehow responsible. I called the prison to check on Charles and found he had been transferred to the state hospital. When I asked what was wrong with him, I was asked in return if I was a relative.

"Can you at least tell me how he's doing? How long he'll be in the hospital?"

"He's not doing well," the voice said before hanging up.

I had a friend in the mayor's office get approval to take Wary to see Charles. But when we got there, he refused to see the dog or me. "Take that mongrel out of here," he yelled. Upon hearing this, Wary began to shake and howl. I quickly got him out of the hospital. He howled all the way home and when I let him in the house, he ran to his cage and wouldn't come out. He refused to eat or drink. After two days of this behavior, I took him to a veterinarian.

"When did he last have water?" the doctor asked. I told him it was yesterday.

"He'll die if he doesn't start drinking soon. We'll give him intravenous fluids and food, but at some point he's got to start eating and drinking on his own. We'll keep him here for a couple of days and see what happens."

When I got home that night there was a message on my answering machine from the hospital: Charles had lapsed into a coma and was not expected to live. The next morning, when I got to the hospital he was dead.

"I'm not a relative," I told them when they asked about removing the body. "Just a friend, an acquaintance. I can't speak for the family."

"But you're the only one who's ever come to see him, who's asked after him."

"I'm sorry," I said. "You'll need to find a relative."

I felt bad about it, but what could I do. He was a guy I knew in high school who had asked for a favor.

A call later that day from the veterinarian announced that Wary was out of the woods. He had begun eating and drinking during the early hours of the morning and he seemed to be fine. Two days later when I picked him up, he jumped in my arms and barked.

Emilio Gomez

La Quema del Diablo

Devils line the cobblestone. In some towns, the entire community gathers around one elaborate, mountainous Beelzebub. Others focus on family reunions, backyard bonfires raging with personal vessels harboring evil. In Antigua, locals and tourists alike parade through ancient squares, coughing up dust from their soles; clapping, shouting, pounding percussions; eyes burning, lighting the sky as they march.

The tradition began in Antigua, and it is here where the festivities remain most elaborate. As La Quema del Diablo edges nearer, the vibrant city's energy intensifies until it becomes palpable. On the morning of the festival, at the height of anticipation, my father and I drive an hour into town to prepare for the cleansing. Over the last few years, it has become our tradition within the broader one.

Papá parks near the Catedral de San José. As always, the plaza outside the famous baroque church flourishes with merchants. Indigenous men and women, dressed in traditional Mayan clothing, gather there to sell kitsch souvenirs and food typical to the region: fresh tortillas, tostadas, chuchitos; atol de elote, horchata; green mangoes served with pepita or sprinkled with salt and showered in lime. Teenagers stand outside portable tents, encouraging all who walk past to peruse their selection of candles bundled by style and by color: tall and thin; thick and short; red, white, yellow, black—exorcists charged with lighting the path for the Virgin Mary.

Clouds parasol the plaza, partly from cars burning oil and partly from the incessant burning of fireworks. I look to the sky and then to my dad, his eyes on the cobblestones, both of us longing for an unreachable warmth. As we cross the street, children my age chase one another, throwing canchinflines and laughing as they explode. One detonates near a five-year-old boy with a face painted red and black. The older kids keep playing, smiling, pockets full of matches, fists full of fire. I extend my hand towards my father's as I quietly observe the game.

We walk past the Arco de Santa Catalina. The air is cooler here, and I can feel a chill running through me as Papá pauses to pray. Behind black metal bars, in the exposed, unlit ruins of the Santa Catalina convent, enormous floats depicting famous biblical scenes and the Seven Sorrows of Mary collect ash, lifeless until Holy Week of next year when supplicant Catholics will shoulder them from one end of Antigua to the other. Papá faces the graveyard of saints as he prays, and I wonder if he will put on the purple robe and raise them once more.

It is across from the ruins that we purchase the devils. A weathered man in a palm leaf hat waits with his hands on his hips, watching us approach the horde of papier-mâché demons, black-bearded and red-skinned, hanging from clothesline or standing beneath it. They aren't supposed to be foreboding—they are caricatures, round-bellied with soft eyes, resembling a twisted take on modern depictions of Saint Nicholas—but their presence is as haunting as the statues shrouded in darkness. I clench my stomach as my father points to the burliest fiend and hands the man fifty quetzales.

The walk back to the car is slow, less purposeful. Papá is exhausted; his eyes are transfixed on a shifting horizon of dusty boots. We stop at the Parque Central, where a woman in a denim apron and red baseball cap stands behind a pushcart, selling shucos. Papá orders two with everything on them, and we sit on a bench facing away from the park. As I remove the repollo from my hot dog, Papá speaks for the first time since he purchased the devil.

"Cómo estás, mi amor?"

"Not too good, Papá," I tell him after a slight hesitation.

"Good," he says. "That is good to hear."

He isn't listening. He is probably thinking of Mamá, his eyes staring beyond him once more, half despondent, half hoping he sees her walking along one of the plazas where they'd spent so many of their weekends. I'm not hungry and Papá isn't looking, but he'll either remain aloof or become irate with me for not appreciating his provisions. I'd rather not to take the risk, so I finish the shuco in silence, the bustle around us becoming progressively louder.

The drive home is more arduous than the walk to the car. I can't help but think of the procession as I look at Papá, his shoulders stooped as if he is bearing the paso with the cross and the Christ on his own, along with all of the sins of the world Jesus placed upon himself. From the back seat, the devil continues to smirk. Papá won't talk to me, so I take solace in the green mountain ranges that surround us. Beyond the bumper-to-bumper traffic and the motorcycles weaving between it, beyond the filthy storefronts and two-story American chains, Guatemala remains "the land of the trees." She is as beautiful as Mamá on the night of her wedding. Maybe that is why Papá has never recovered—there is nowhere to drive and escape her visage.

At the gate that leads to our community, Papá retrieves a cigarette from the center console and lights it. The guard on duty sees us from afar. He exits the guardhouse, waving a friendly hand my father doesn't return. The guard is young, clothed in combat boots and a militant uniform. As he hurries to manually open the gate, the shotgun slung on his back bounces behind him. Papá releases a heavy sigh, then slowly drives past the guard, his eyes narrowed and facing the road.

"Estamos bien," he turns and says to me. I'm not sure if it's a question or a plea for solidarity: *Hold me accountable, like all is well, because I am falling apart.* I nod slowly, and we turn onto our street. My uncles are standing outside, laughing with beers in their hands, oblivious to my cousins playing around them or the sadness their brother is attempting to cloak. We park against the sidewalk, and they raise their bottles in our direction, my mother's brother approaching with one for my dad. I walk into the house where my aunts are frying buñuelos, and I help them stir the warm ponche de frutas before retreating upstairs to gather my thoughts.

In the top drawer of the desk in my room, there is a white, leather-bound Bible my mother gifted me the day I was born. My name is engraved in gold on the cover. I grab the Bible and lie on my bed, retrieving a photograph from within. In it, my father smiles deeply, his skin wrinkling at the ends of his eyes. He wears a black tuxedo and a mustache. My mother holds faded, fuchsia ranunculi. They face one another before an arch decorated with flowers where a priest stands, slightly turned towards my mother. "Till death do us part," I imagine him saying.

"Till death do us part," I imagine her lying.

Outside, I could hear the clamor that will comprise the ignition. For weeks, families in my neighborhood have been gathering trash, books, clothes, and furniture. Satan hides beneath beds and in closets; he possesses gifts, haunts jewelry and dolls. I peer through the blinds above my headboard. My uncles are carrying the offerings to the road, along with fresh wood to light the fire. My father stands in the dust, smoking a cigarette, stuffing the demon with ignition. The night is approaching.

Tia Tina calls to me from the steps. Outside, the men are dusting off their hands and dispersing. It is time to eat. I look at the picture once more, at the rapture in Papá's smile. I put the Bible back in the desk where I found it and stuff the picture in the back pocket of my jeans. "Ya voy," I call as I open my door and walk to the dining room.

Three rectangular folding tables covered with plaid manteles have been connected to seat all of the adults: uncles and aunts, Abuelo y Abuela, older first and second cousins and some of their spouses. Mamá's family joins us each holiday. They never distanced themselves from me or Papá—after all, when Mamá moved in with a gringo she met waiting tables, she left all of us here. The tables are overflowing with food and with chatter. Even Papá appears to be happy, laughing and engaged in discussion, unaware of me as I enter the room. Tia Tina calls me again and hands me a plastic plate full of food. Between the living room and dining room are the round tables with plain red manteles reserved for the children. I walk over and find an open seat with some of the others.

My table is speaking of school and of crushes, but my mind is on Mamá. La Quema is a cleanse to prepare us for the Feast of the Immaculate Conception, a celebration of the sinless life and Immaculate Conception of the Blessed Virgen María—María, the name given to half of Central America, including my mother. I used to wonder if she felt the pressure to live up to her perfect namesake, to be the immaculate wife and mother and to cheerfully emanate grace under all circumstances. I pitied her, absolved her of her sins against Papá and me—it helped slow the tears on the sleepless nights. But Papá has never recovered, and lately pity has been turning to rage. While Mary held the dying Jesus in her bloodied arms, María crossed hers, leaving me orphaned.

As I clench my fist and feel for the photo, the adults begin to rise. I follow them outside, where the devil is waiting. Against the twilight, his eyes glow, and I shake. My aunts light candles and recite prayers to the Virgin Mary. My uncles use lighter fluid and matches to begin the conflagration. Once it is raging, Papá extends his arms, violently grabs the deceiver by his feet and horns. He suspends him over the fire and begins to condemn him: "For gang violence; for a corrupt, oppressive government; for alcoholism that destroys families and for families that separate without excuses, where drugs and alcohol were not present and where money was not a problem; for mothers who abandon their children like cowardly men do, who start new lives in new countries with new husbands; for villains parading as heroes, forsaking with grins, disregarding those who—"

His lips continue to move, but I can't hear the words. Moisture builds in my palms and crawls to the tips of my fingers. My face is flushed, scarlet like the demon covered in flames. I look at the crowd, try to imagine Papá smiling beneath his darkened eyes, his back broken with laughter and not with grief. To envision my mother, weary, walking towards him, grabbing his hand and kissing his cheek, planting her feet on native soil. In the city below and in neighboring towns, fiends have been burning for over an hour. The sky and the streets are shadowed by an oppressive smoke. My eyes are on fire, tears beginning to well. I wipe them with a shaking hand, and when no one is looking, I walk to the embers and surrender the image.

E. Reid

The Holy Family

The miracle of their meeting was no miracle. It was merely a meeting. It did so happen that it was at church, so you might expect their relationship got started off on a particularly holy foot. But so much depends upon the church. Maddie was a long timer at Pine Ridge non-denominational, almost a decade at the little liberal church that was quite an anomaly in Laurie, Tennessee. She loved the church because, unlike at its Baptist counterparts, one didn't have to believe in a personal savior to be a member. You could just believe that belief in general helps you to live a better life. Full of artsy and teacher types, services at Pine Ridge were one part sing-along to the songs of Joni Mitchell and the Indigo Girls and one part conversation about our role in caring for the earth and its inhabitants.

For Laurie, it was already outrageously diverse, and indeed weird, but Pine Ridge was always seeking ways to invite more in. The church had some success wooing a few local cowgirls, loner rural ranch women with their own bit of property, workin' their horses and lovin' their dogs. That's how Mab came into the picture. She walked in wearing those dark colored jeans from the Sears catalog, with bright orange threaded seams and fabric so thick it could stand itself up and walk the dog. She wore cowboy boots, of course, and a button-down shirt—no, snaps—that made a delightful popping sound the first time Maddie grabbed them.

It didn't take long for the two of them to find each other. Maddie was leading a chorus of "Closer to Fine" from the pulpit and Mab sang out Amy Ray's part in such a smoky rich alto, it was all Maddie could do to keep herself upright. After the service, she walked right up to Mab and said, "Hey there, how'd a country bumpkin like you learn to sing like that?"

"Juilliard," Mab said, and smirked, then was silent the way cowgirls are silent.

Maddie invited her to lunch. Beer got her talking, a little, but it was more of the campfire in her eyes than anything she said that won Maddie over. In fact, the moment Maddie thought the phrase, "campfire in her eyes," she was gone. She was an aspiring writer, and getting the right word was something close to ecstasy. She felt a red coal glow inside, hot enough to toast a marshmallow a golden chewy brown. She said, "I feel warm inside," for she felt the incessant need to verbalize her observations. Mab smiled and flashed a brushfire across the table.

In retrospect, such instant connection, and use of the metaphor of fire, does suggest the miraculous, or at least the really great serendipitous way life sometimes unfolds. In secret, Maddie felt it was a miracle, but she called it natural for it was part of her worldview that there was no deity to perform personal acts of wonder, but there were inexplicable acts of nature itself. The way the sky could rise up from the ground in a horizon of red beauty and then vanish in blackness. The way things could come to you right when you need them, like a scholarship for school or a part-time job, or just the right song on the radio. No, the first two could be explained by positional status, being broke but connected to social capital by means of her middle-class community. But, the miracle—or, no, natural wonder—of just the right song playing on the radio in just the right moment, that was a happening. The way, for instance, "Chelsea Morning" played on their first morning together, and the sun really did come in like butterscotch and stuck to all their senses (and they did talk in present tenses!) and the bowl of oranges sparkled and the cat purred and there was colored glass light everywhere like jewels.

One might wonder what actually could rise to the descriptor of "miracle" if even this happening did not warrant the label. No doubt Joni Mitchell is celestially connected. But this is a good question to hold onto for later. For what was to happen was nothing short of extraordinary.

The next morning at the ranch they sat on the front porch, on a swing no less, and watched the spring trees feather into morning. A soft rain drizzled, and the birds sang their hearts out. All the dogs and cats curled around their legs and laps. They clutched their hot cups and each other. Maddie's breasts and belly pushed at the seams of the too-small night shirt. Mab's stocky strong legs pressed into the stone floor and pushed them rocking on the swing.

"I hear a creek!" Maddie exclaimed.

"Yes, over there." Mab pointed.

Beside the creek was a weeping willow, enormous tree-length metal pipes hanging from its branches. Their song was itself a deep alto.

"You'll have to go stand inside them," Mab said quietly, "when it stops raining."

"Stand inside what?"

"They're a healing station."

Maddie could not resist and padded right off across the wet grass in the soft rain and stood in the space made by the four pipes. Two wooden bars hung from a hook. She dislodged them and struck the pipes timidly then with bright confident taps. Then she stood and felt a wave of sound envelop her, a sound felt by her entire body, stomach to toes, and continuing long after her ears quit hearing the overlapping tones. She felt the vibration of air, the movement of the earth, her own blood. She stood and breathed until there was stillness, and then when she walked, she felt the vibration deep in her own chest.

"I believe I will carry that with me the rest of the day," she said.

Mab's smile revealed an unexpected shyness, and pleasure.

"I've never seen such a thing." Maddie looked around the porch and now noticed a rainbow of bark holding chimes of gradually decreasing lengths, like pipes in an organ. She saw bamboo fitted into the bottom of a gourd. Her fingers twitched waiting to tap it, to hear its purpose. "Wait 'til you see the trees," Mab said.

This was Maddie's introduction to the world of Mab—the musical world of Mab, whom she discovered made actual instruments in her spare time, but only of materials found there on her place and around town. Bark from cedar trees and oak. Bamboo from the creekside. Metal bars found in the Laurie recyclery. Maddie was to discover butterfly wings in the empty upturned shells of turtles, and rocks tucked into the nooks of the branches, rocks with deep eyes formed by nature's drips over thousands of years, mostly eyes, but sometimes round mouths that sang "oohs" from their birdlike perches. She was to hear the call of the Mourning Dove, the Hoot Owl, the Cardinal and see their red bodies like berries on the beige branches of winter and the yellow-green branches of spring. She was to hear the loud cry of the yellow barn cat, like a screech or a banshee calling for milk or for touch. She was to watch the dogs relax into an open gate across a horse pasture and sit sphinx-like on the porch watching Chickadees and Tufted Titmice eat the seed from the feeders and squirrels chase each other's tails and smell, and smell, and smell, their necks green with horse dung where they rolled in bliss and carried the pasture home with them much like Maddie carried the vibration inside. What a world for dogs!

Maddie lost her words in such glory. So alive was the external world outside her own fertile mind, and so alive was the strong woman holding her tender hand in a hand at once calloused from work and delicate from music, with the subtlety and passion of a Chopin phrase (oh, when she heard Mab play the piano!) so alive became everything outside herself, whereas she had lived her thirty odd years to this point finding her own inner world the most interesting of all. The mundane exterior life of lesson plans and dishes, the carefulness of people, the expectedness, the way miracles happened inside the heart and mind, but never in the hard light of day, never in the material world which ticked on like a clock, and the only thing to do had been to see its potential, to hold her own counsel. She was a cheerful and boisterous part of humanity, ready with a song and dance or a crystalline thought, a life observation, a bit of gentle mischief. You could count on Maddie to tuck her brown bob behind her ear when she really listened to you. You could count on her to sing a Barbra Streisand song when the room grew too dull. You could count on her to show up for work almost on time, but do it every day. She counted on these traits—the social kind—to make easy and lively the gap between inner and outer lives. The longing inside for miracles to be true, for people to be unexpected, to be seen.

She was lonely. She saw so much magic. She talked to the people, the many beings in her mind and body, so incessantly that she even carried on the conversations in her sleep. She talked in her sleep with intensity. And sometimes walked! As though in the dark hours her body was willing to act as though what was inside was really true. In the morning, she'd find towels moved into the center of the floor, glasses rearranged, an apple standing in solitary beauty on the windowsill framed in an environment of green yard light.

For all she talked, how could there be so much unsaid? She knew her talking was in a way to run circles around the mystery. She could not say what was felt inside, what was seen and known, could not say it with her tongue in words that made sense in the external world. Words could only approximate meaning, every once in a while get close, and until the day she discovered writing, she had no way to connect the world.

Then there was the day that writing broke in like a "Chelsea Morning," like a "Mississippi Goddamn" and a "How Great Thou Art." (Then sings my soul!) She took an evening writing class and her teacher said words that connected. You must have both tension and authority of voice at the beginning of a story. Tension means something is at stake: there is a question, a lurking. Authority of voice is the confidence of the writer to really tell it: to rise up in language on the page. That's what will make a reader trust you and want to go along.

Maddie was taken by the command to be authoritative on the page—and about a question no less, not an answer! To be authoritative about the mystery itself and to be confident in her writing of it. Confidence as a necessity, instead of a privilege owned by those with all the answers.

She took her pen and hid in the bathroom stall during break. Pants down, on a scrap of an old bill pulled from her purse, she wrote: *My parts don't grow at the same pace. My bones grow faster than my muscles, and the way they pull at the joints makes me howl.* She breathed, huffed the air. A little boy appeared on the page, and his overweight mother, depressed and sickly. And Jesus himself showed up. And there was a merry-go-round ride and the boy saw blurs of color, his mother's pink face, and a cloud of dancing trees. And suddenly there was a bridge! Maddie could have wept with the miracle of it, of words that created life that lived outside herself.

She did weep, and laugh. She married writing and scorned lovers who would take the place of her new passion, her only true passion. She secluded herself in darkness and in dawn and wrote story after story. She went to school to study craft. She acted as though it was about ambition, another degree, she could teach or publish or hold community writing workshops, but it was really about being alive inside.

So now you may understand the wonder of Mab's ranch in Maddie's heart, and the wonder of Mab herself, who lived the outside life as daringly as Maddie lived the inside. It took Maddie's words right away, for where was the need to try to say, to bridge, when here she was in the pulsing world, when there was after all no separation. She was amazed just to be, as though she had become a character in her own story and magic was real.

Even so, she could not stay wordless forever. Words came knocking and pressing at her. She was afraid to write them lest waking up the words would shatter the world she now inhabited. Before, words had only been a conduit, an attempt to cross over into this, so now what would they be? The writers all said that every story was about longing, and what was her longing now? Oh, it was like the old question of why God created the world when He (or She) already had everything, was *God,* for Heaven's sake. What more could be needed? But, they say, God was so full of love that She just had to keep finding ways to express it, and to really manifest it. That Love beget creation. And even for an agnostic nature worshipper, this story always was a delight. And here she was herself, my God, writing, not to scale a broken world but to overflow with wholeness.

So it was that one day, after she had fully moved in with Mab, and they had lived a lifetime in just a few months, she went upstairs in the ranch house, and she made herself a place to write. She sat at the window gazing at the tops of the trees and the bottoms of the clouds, feeling the vibration of her lover in her workshop down below. She wrote these words on a blank unlined page. "God is love." Or she wrote, "So much depends on a red wheelbarrow." Or she wrote, "In the beginning the word was made flesh," or whatever image that came to her that day. The image was itself replete, it was itself the meaning. It was itself love and mystery and God—the red wheelbarrow, the ineffable, not the description around the edges, the attempt to cross over into the thing, but *The Thing* itself. She filled with such ringing, such vibration, such light and darkness and sky and earth, she moved like particles of everything from her chair down the stairs to the kitchen where Mab stood in silence, crying, herself with no words, but a piece of tree she'd sanded and rubbed until she found the shape of a bear in the wood, and the shape of a crow and the shape of water and of fire, and she'd burned the word "Love" right in the middle in rippling letters in a hand becoming particle even as it held its tool.

That is when they both, at the same time, exploded like a star being born, a super nova, a Big Bang. They clutched each other's bodies. They were naked. They were warm skin. They were tongues and teeth. They were fingers and flesh and bellies and broad shoulders and tender skin. They were exploded in pieces so fine their bodies became heat itself. They became a river and a current of fire. They became stone and then exploded into air. Their house shook with the velocity, the energy, the cosmic event of their lovemaking—so perfect, so real and surreal, so magical and natural, so bursting and melting, and when they came back to their forms, reincarnated, heaving, cold, they wrapped up in blankets and made a cave, and said nothing for days, until Maddie emerged from the bathroom one morning and said, "I think I'm pregnant."

Oddly, in this, the most miraculous of all their happenings, neither treated it as something unusual. They took it as a natural outcome of what they'd already exploded through. Maddie did joke in her ideological way that a baby produced by the Big Bang ought to reconcile for once and for all, without a shadow of a doubt, the creationists' and evolutionists' debate about the origin of the earth, the universe, "man," and everything. The answer, of course, was that it was all true, both at the same time, and everything in between. Her rising, earth-shaped belly bore witness.

Maddie was surprised and not surprised by the changes in her body. She became even fleshier, her breasts tender and sensitized to the slightest touch. A puff of air in her low-buttoned shirt. Mab would come and place her hand across the growing belly. "You have a beautiful belly," she'd say each time with a regularity which caused Maddie to see herself more like a beautiful, happy Buddha than the sumo wrestler she sometimes felt like.

They picked paint colors for the spare room, and they talked about baby names. The typical things. Mab spent extra time in her workshop, hand fashioning a cradle from the shell of a tree. She'd been chiseling out the center for weeks and carving rockers for the base so their little creation could rock gently into each night.

Maddie, for her part, was painting a forested mural in the bedroom, evergreens and deciduous trees together. Great peaks of Western mountains towered over gentle Appalachian rounds, streams tucked into ancient stone, and cozy Hobbit nooks and snowy peaks stood sentry. It was the season for canning, and they both began to sauce and put away all the pears, apples, and carrots they could find.

At church, they were heartily congratulated and their silence on the origin of life was taken as a certain privacy some women carried with the intimate matters of their lives. Why would it matter anyway, because soon there would be a loved child and a holy family, and the church members would take turns offering precious gifts and adoration.

Interestingly, the place of first reaction to the couple's happy news came from Mab's parents. Traditional folk, but avid cable TV watchers, they knew the possible options for two women who wanted a baby. They were not so willing to tolerate the mystery. They started with innocuous questions like, "How is your money holding up? I know it's an expensive process." But Mab and Maddie only laughed and said they were fine on that front. They asked about genetic history, and Mab said, "Only the best." They asked about bureaucracy, and there was none. Finally, they got it into their combined minds that Maddie had been unfaithful and that Mab was making the best of a bad situation. But they remained silent on this theory and just watched.

"Your parents are giving me the stink eye again," Maddie would often say. But finally, they seemed to surrender their curiosity, for the mounting excitement of a grandchild took over, and they truthfully adored Maddie and her strange ways, and so they filled the house with gifts. When the baby was born, the grandparents held her and sang quiet little songs their grandparents had sung to them. The newborn infant had an official name, Micah Irene, after a great grandmother, and as it happened, also a great uncle, but Mab and Maddie took to calling her "M&M," a sweet morsel, a tiny melting bit of Heaven.

M&M was born on a Tuesday morning before dawn. Maddie had left for the thirty-minute drive to town and turned around in the dark to come back for the look of Mab's eyes. M&M came knocking in the most delicate way, like a feather tickling Maddie from the inside, and then a great gush of water breaking. Mab toweled the floor and her own hair fresh from the shower and loaded Maddie into the farm truck for the drive to the ER.

"Mab, honey," Maddie said. "If I have this baby in this truck, you must promise me to incinerate it."

"The baby?" Mab asked, meanly.

"The truck! You evil thing." But she laughed.

"Honey," Mab said, "this is no time to get one of your germophobic fits. You're going to just have to let nature take its course."

As if timed, a massive contraction struck like the squeezing of the hand of God. Breathing through clenched teeth, Maddie lit out in short bursts: "I. Am. Not. Germ. O. Phobic. I. Just. Don't. Want to. Clean up my own. Insides. From this. Damn. Truck!" The contraction passed and she followed with, "I mean, what would you use anyway? Comet? Bleach?"

"How about Goo Gone, honey?"

Maddie laughed and felt the little one start to come into a world full of laughter. Luckily, they pulled up to the ER entrance, and the rest was a tumble of angry cow-like vocalizations, hand wringing and pushing, pushing through pain like a chainsaw to a daisy. But later, Maddie's memory would be the laughter and she'd always tell M&M, "Babygirl, you were born into joy."

It was true that M&M had an unusually fine sparkle in her eyes right from the beginning. In fact, it was just one eye that sparkled like a single star in a midnight sky, a dark eye that winked at the edges, a little crinkled right from the start, and looked deeply, darkly into your face and laughed. Her other eye, the right one, opened wide and fresh like a baby eye, full of light and wonder, the eye that first filled with tears or watched the barn cats playing like it was seeing a miracle. In this way, she had an unusual appearance—not disfigured or uncomfortable—just a little slant, like she saw things slanted and her face followed suit. It gave her at once the look of deep mischief and wide wonder, which if one didn't expect utter symmetry in a face, gave her a beautiful and wild look, quite a wiggly contradiction.

The only times her eyes matched were when she laughed the family laugh, the great belly laugh cackle they all shared. Then her tiny face burst with joy and was utter sunshine more than eyes, nose, and mouth. She had a heart bursting quality in that face, which seems appropriate for a child of the Big Bang. In her older childhood her words dug right to the source of things, that wide right eye capturing your heart and that left glinting eye saying the secret your social words obscured.

"Oh, child!" Mab would sigh in such an episode. One day, Mab had just come from the tractor, her muck boots plastered with grass and her hands pulling off their leather work gloves. She fetched a beer from the fridge, pried off its top, and took a long drink. M&M watched this common ritual from her seat at the table where she'd been filling a page with squiggly lines in rainbow colors. Then Maddie came in from the back bedroom with a cloud of vacuum dust and just stared at that bronze, beer drinking woman.

M&M looked at Maddie with her glinting eye and said, "Mama, I can't tell if you're coveting her beer or her body." Then she looked with that eye of wonder, and the astonished parents couldn't tell if she was being wicked, naïve, or precocious, or if she even knew what she was saying.

M&M could have meant that she saw Maddie's desire for a beer—which she didn't drink so often because of what the calories would do to her already plump physique. Or, if Maddie was looking at Mab's body and wishing she could indulge and still look like that—muscular and cocksure on her two strong legs, hips jutting just to the side. Or, if Maddie was looking at that body and wanting to touch it, to "love on it," as she'd say, and couldn't because their little one was present, or because they were in work mode, or because they didn't touch that way as much as they used to. Life was just too hard and busy to surrender into the Passion on a daily basis. But it tugged at them, and they sometimes watched each other's bodies quietly and privately, catching each other now and then, but never speaking their thoughts.

"Oh, child," Mab sighed. M&M returned to her page and started to make long lightning zigzags which revealed her drawing to be of a rainbow rainstorm.

Maddie walked to the fridge and took out a beer. She pried off the top, cocked her hips, and took back the top third in one chug. Mab grabbed the seam of her jeans with her brown fingers and pulled her hips an inch closer so that her shoulders were pulled back, and her pelvis pressed forward, so slightly, but they looked at each other, and there was enough heat in that moment to last them another month. M&M. Their little lightning storm. Crackling in some innocent truth or mischief when it was needed.

"You speak words close to the bone," Maddie would say, and Mab would pat their daughter's head with a pleasing thump. M&M would either be silent, or she'd say, as she did on this day, "Well, someone has to."

Maddie conjured this image years later when she started trying to write the story of her family, when she struggled for bravery in her voice and pen to tell it true. The story she was maybe always meant to write. She pictured her fierce and tender child, and she wrote these words:

On the morning our baby was born, I drove absurdly, without knowledge, through the freezing dark just to see the look in Mab's eyes. That is all, the look. I had left for work to no stars, the long drive over the hills and pastures, past the McGee house, the gradual appearance of human civilization, the factories, the churches, and then town. But this morning I stopped at the white gate and circled back and returned home. Then, under a round moon half-veiled in cloud, this look and this scene—my unexpected return, the crunch of the tires in the gravel, the back door sliding wide, soft hands on the heads of dogs, footfalls gentle to the bathroom, the sound of the fan, the fine mist, the just-combed hair, wet and pressed to the head, the eyes full of surprise but no fear, bright, and the heaving of our hearts.

This is the morning we birthed our little girl fresh into the world like a sprout in the garden. Like a moonbeam into our home, a babe in the manger. Though we did make it to the hospital, thank God, that moment was her arrival. M&M. Our holy child. Attended by two moms, two dogs and three cats, a white mule, uncountable deer, songbirds, turkey vultures, cows, horses, butterflies, and squirrels. Down the road a goat, over the hill some peafowl, and a few fat hogs.

This isn't a new story. In fact, it is very old. But it is ours, and it is immaculate.

Ilan Mochari

Shirley's Sticky Sole (1982)

Shirley ran to greet her father when she heard his unmistakable knock: nine whacks, with pauses prior to the fourth and seventh. The pattern was how he revealed himself, he explained, so if one day he forgot his keys, and she were home alone, she'd know it was safe to open. Now that his girlfriend, Elodia, was living with them, Shirley was seldom home alone. But he still knocked nine times every weekday afternoon, as if to remind Shirley of the procedure—or remind her of something else.

He knelt by his briefcase, snapped it open, and handed her a mimeographed poem, "The Monkeys," by Marianne Moore. While Shirley studied it, he went into the kitchen and whispered to Elodia. Then, in a louder voice, he told Elodia that he and Shirley would be back by dinnertime. Elodia smacked him on the tush. He whistled his favorite jazz song, the one about coming home.

In the hallway, Shirley pushed the elevator button, but her father opened the heavy door that led to the stairwell. They climbed down five flights of sticky steps and exited via the basement laundry room, passing through a plume of detergent-scented steam. Their street, Almond Avenue, was busy as ever. Trucks and buses sped by in both directions; parents and children strode hand-in-hand on the narrow sidewalk. At the subway entrance, her father lifted her up, so they'd only need one token to pass through the turnstiles.

When they were aboard the train to Brooklyn, she took "The Monkeys" out of her jeans pocket. She asked him what one of the big words, *astringently*, meant. He told her to look it up for herself. A few minutes later he asked how *she'd* have written the poem. For example, what if she'd called it "The Spiders"—and used facts from her library books? "I'll think about it," she said.

They were quiet for a while, leaning into each other whenever the train shrieked to a stop. He began whistling the coming-home song again. "Were you a substitute today?" she asked. She suspected the answer was yes, since he was in a good mood. "Ninth grade algebra," he declared. He said he loved the texture of chalk in his fingers, how the rapid writing made him feel like a musician, matching his clacks on the blackboard to the trumpet notes in his head. Sure, he was excited to be the new assistant principal at P.S. 1821—but he missed being in a classroom every day.

When they were outside again, he picked her up and set her down, feet-first, on the roof of a parked car. She climbed onto his shoulders, tucking her fingers into the collar of his corduroy sports jacket—the one he'd bought after becoming assistant principal. In the street, six boys were playing football. They shouted strange phrases and numbers at each other: *Kenny, I'm open!* and *One, one-thousand, two, one-thousand, three, one-thousand!* Whenever a car came, the boys loped to the sidewalk and stood next to a box radio blasting music.

Shirley stared at the brick building across the road, where Marianne Moore used to live. The fire escape zigzagged down the front, like five capital Z's in a stack. She imagined climbing it and reaching the roof. The red bricks had faded—they were almost pink. The sky above was bright blue, like the V-necks Elodia wore for her job at the hospital. "If I live on the fifth floor, you can live above me," she said.

"On the roof?" he said.

She sighed. "The sky's blue, like a boy's room. So you're *up there*," she said.

"I see," he replied. "Well, I can certainly picture you following in Marianne Moore's footsteps."

"Do you love Marianne Moore?" asked Shirley.

"Yes."

"More than *my* mom?" she asked.

"No," he said. "Not more than Elodia, either."

"Why didn't you name me Marianne?"

"We've been over this." He turned his head from left to right, following the football as it spiraled in the air.

"Tell me again."

"*I* wanted to name you Marianne. But your mother, may she rest in peace, wanted your name to start with *Sh*," he said, making a shushing sound. "Her intent was to honor *her* mother—your maternal grandmother—whose name was Shandra."

"I think you secretly *wish* I was a boy," said Shirley, also making a shushing sound.

He grabbed her arms and flipped her forward, pressing her upsidedown into the braced front of his body. Shirley shook with laughter. Her sneakers slapped the sidewalk as she landed, completing her somersault. Her father took off his sports jacket, folded it, and placed it on the roof of the car. "Hey!" he shouted at the kids in the street, clapping his hands. "Five seconds, let me see it."

One of them tossed him the ball. He spun it around in his hand until his fingers pressed the white string—a pile of capital I's, like the spine of a skeleton.

"Try holding it," he whispered.

It was too wide for Shirley's grip.

"Come on, old man," shouted one of the boys.

He stepped forward and threw. The ball soared over their heads, wobbling, and smashed the box radio, cracking the cassette tray. The music stopped.

"Sorry," he shouted. He grabbed her by the waist and picked her up. A wet wad of gum, glued to her left sneaker, stretched into a thin white line before breaking at the center.

He ran to the corner, holding her in his arms. Over his shoulder, she saw two of the boys turning knobs on the radio. The others chased him. He crossed the street and veered into the entrance of a delicatessen. He took her into the men's restroom and locked the door. The armpits of his dress shirt were soaked. She sat on the closed lid of the toilet as he paced and caught his breath. "Can you stay here with the door locked and count to sixty?" he said.

She nodded. He told her he'd be right back—he just wanted to apologize to the boys and make sure they weren't really angry.

When he left, shutting the door behind him, she gazed at the corners of the ceiling and the windowsill. She was searching for spiders or webs in their usual places. Finding none, she pinched at the gum stuck to her sneaker. There was a knock on the door—not *his*. She tilted her ear toward the keyhole and heard a medley of men's voices. Then she heard a voice that she recognized, and a familiar pattern of knocking. She opened. "Where's the other knocker?" she asked.

"Probably eating his coleslaw," he said. "Let's skedaddle."

Back on the train, she reread "The Monkeys." When they were almost home, he cursed and punched the seat. "God fucking dammit all to hell!" he shouted.

She looked at him. He blushed, rolled his eyes, and let out a short laugh. "Ah, Shirl—don't tell Elodia, okay?"

"That you cursed?" she asked.

Now he laughed hard, like he did whenever she tickled him in his most ticklish spot—the back of his knees. The other passengers stared at them.

When he was able to speak again, he said, "No, you can tell her I cursed. She's heard it before, believe me. But don't tell her I broke the radio, and that the kids chased us, and that I hid you in the men's room."

"What if she asks how you lost your sports jacket?"

He stared at the roof of the subway car for a moment, then looked in her eyes. "Tell her we took it to the cleaners," he said, winking.

She nodded.

Then he reached for her left foot and took off her sneaker. He dug his nails into the sole, doing his best to pick at and peel away the drying wad.

Katya Cengel

A Palm Tree in the Ruins

Marko lights a cigarette. There are so many English words he has forgotten. So many others he never knew. Smoking buys him time. Why did he volunteer to translate for his father in the first place, he wonders. Pride, curiosity, filial duty, it could have been any of those. Or all of them. Holding the cigarette in his right hand, he flips his laptop open with his left. He pulls up a document with notes he made earlier.

"I can give this to you," he says to the American journalist sitting next to him. "I asked my father questions earlier and put it here."

She glances at the document. The English words written in bullet points listing his father's major sculptures. It is all there. But the journalist doesn't want bullet points. Marko realizes this when she finishes reading the document and looks up at him. She nods and then bites her lower lip. Expecting. Wanting.

She is okay looking. Tall and slim, probably in her early forties, like Marko, with a shy smile and large dark eyes. He isn't attracted to her, but there is that electricity of being with a foreign woman. One who is dependent on him to understand not only what is being said but the long history behind those words.

"I need quotes, sound bites, something colorful. Not facts and figures," she says.

He nods his head, takes a drag on his cigarette. Marko looks at the document again as if it will somehow translate into fluid words he can offer her.

"Let's start with his major sculpture," she says.

She turns to Marko's father, Josip.

"What inspired you to make a Muhammad Ali monument in Bosnia?"

Josip smiles, patiently waiting for Marko to translate her words. Putting the words in Croatian is easier than changing Croatian to English. Marko translates her question quickly. Josip's smile widens with understanding. He is in his late sixties but still active. He doesn't smoke, and although Marko is hesitant to mention it for fear of invoking the evil eye, is healthy. Josip's words are not as beautiful as what he makes with his hands, but they are thoughtful. By the time Marko is through with them they are clunky and utilitarian.

"He wants to make something for the people," Marko says.

The journalist scribbles in her notebook. Her eyes focus on the paper only briefly before they once again bore into Marko. Questions shoot out of her mouth, one after another.

"What does Muhammad Ali mean to the people?"

"How did he choose the pose?"

"Does the material he used have any significance?"

"How long did it take him? Why did he decide to make it so small?"

Marko stubs his cigarette in the ashtray. He can answer the questions without asking his father, they are easy. But he knows that is not what she wants. He reads the *New York Post*. He notices how the people quoted in the articles talk a lot about very little. She is like those journalists, hungry for his father's words. He asks his father for answers and translates them back before his father is finished, relying on his memory as much as his father's replies.

"Ali is a fighter for justice, Bosnian people like that. He wanted Ali to stand, not sit. The bronze shines like gold. He spent two weeks. Small, so people must look closer."

The answers seem to satisfy her. While she is busy writing, Marko glances around the café. It isn't a venue he usually visits, too expensive, too formal, too far from his neighborhood. His father chose it for the attentive waiters and sweets, neither of which seem to interest the journalist. Almost every table is taken. People are talking, sipping their coffee, smoking. Marko had to bring the laptop here because of the American. He needed the computer to show her the document and to look up unfamiliar words. If she wasn't here the laptop wouldn't be, either. Marko doesn't blame her. The language barrier prevents a relaxed atmosphere.

Marko had forgotten what Americans are like. The constant chasing of something. Bosnians are productive, but they know how to live. Americans treat even their pastimes like work, with goals and tight schedules. Marko remembers that from the two-week computer programing course his company sent him to in San Francisco before he was a husband and father. All the Americans he met talked about how much they worked, bragging about double shifts and sixty-hour work weeks. It was one of the reasons he decided not to overstay his visa. That and his father.

Marko loves both his parents, but he is closest to his father. When he needs advice, he asks Josip. Marko often finds his father in his studio painting or sculpting. His father continues working while he listens, nodding every once in a while. When Marko is finished talking, Josip stops his work and focuses on his son. He looks at Marko for a long time before speaking. When he says something, it's often an anecdote about his own life. By the time he is done Marko knows what he will do. He doesn't always tell his father his decision. Instead, they start talking about art, and his father's hands once again return to the work they were doing before Marko interrupted.

Marko hasn't talked to his father about leaving. It's the one thing he doesn't want to work out with him. He knows what life his father has chosen for himself. So many of Marko's friends have already gone. Bosnians are wanted in many places for their strong work ethic and skills, especially computer skills like Marko's. At least that is what Emil tells him. His childhood friend left last year for France and already has a French girlfriend and a fancy flat. Emil floods Marko's phone with video messages showing Emil stuffing himself in restaurants, "working" at cafés and kissing his girlfriend under the Eiffel Tower and other famous landmarks. Marko isn't impressed by the videos. He is focused on the figures. The triple digit salary figures. The political figures who attempt to speak for the majority of the population.

His father's voice interrupts Marko's thoughts. Josip is asking a question that is easy to translate, nothing the journalist will want to quote.

"He would like to show you some of his work. Do you have time?" Marko asks.

"Yes, I would love that," she says.

Marko prepares to shut down his laptop, taking one last look at his email before he closes it. It is still there in his inbox. An email from a money management company in Berlin offering him a job he had forgotten he had even applied for, one he never told Anya about because he never thought he would get it. It is a systems analysis gig that would pay twice what he is currently making as the head of IT at a small Catholic college. They would even cover moving expenses.

The journalist stuffs her notebook and mini recorder in her back pocket. Josip picks up the slim briefcase he carries everywhere even though he has been retired for five years. His father has been looking forward to this meeting for weeks, ever since the email arrived.

Hello Josip,

Do you speak English? I'm using AI translation, so I apologize for the bad text. I am an American journalist writing a story about the Balkans' unusual monuments. Is there a day in the last week of August we can meet?

An American journalist traveling to the Balkans to write about the area's unusual monuments. Bob Marley in Serbia. Rocky Balboa, Tarzan, Muhammad Ali, and a one-time Playboy model scattered about the region. Neither Josip nor Marko could resist the chance to talk to an American journalist, a woman from the country where everything happens, where all the music and movie trends begin, where everyone wants to be. Even if Marko doesn't want to go there anymore, America and Americans still fascinate him. That is why Marko is here translating.

Outside the cafe as they walk to the car Marko can tell his father wants to talk to the journalist. Marko purposefully walks far enough ahead to make that difficult. It isn't that he doesn't like translating, just that he doesn't want to slow down their excursion with small talk. The journalist is silent for once.

Marko has to move his son Luka's car seat out of the middle of the back seat so the journalist can sit comfortably. Luka poos yellow messes that spill out of even the thickest diapers. Still, there is something about the baby. The way he grips Marko's finger and seems to almost laugh when Marko tickles his belly. He is so small, so breakable. Last month when Marko was carrying Luka down the apartment stairs he nearly slipped, catching himself and Luka just in time. Marko refused to carry his son after that. Anya thought he was being lazy. He couldn't tell her about his fear of failing her and Luka. Anya would laugh and point out that she works too. But her income covers barely a third of their expenses.

Josip arranges himself in the passenger seat. Once Marko is behind the wheel he heads toward the hills and the massive cross at the top. It is at the largest hill that Josip carved two of the Stations of the Cross, part of the fourteen-step Catholic devotion commemorating Jesus' last day. Most artists were only hired to carve one of the stations leading up the hill, but Josip knew the man commissioning the work, so he was given two.

When he was a teenager Marko liked to visit the half-dozen statues and frescos his father carved around the city. He would stand by them, sometimes below them, reminding himself who he was and what his father had done. It made him feel like he belonged. He dreamed of taking his son to the same spots when he was old enough and telling him his grandfather had carved them with his own hands. Luka is too young now, not talking yet. Not even walking. If he took Luka to Western Europe his son wouldn't grow up in a city crafted by their family, in a city where their language is spoken. He would grow up in an unrelated land where his parents would always be foreigners.

They are almost to the hill when his father gestures with his hand, reminding Marko to tell the journalist that he carved the doves in the top of the church spire. Marko doesn't need to be reminded. The birds are one of his favorites.

Marko pulls over. "He carved those," he says, pointing to the church spire where three doves are arranged in a circle.

"Wow, those are beautiful, when did he do that?"

Marko knows the answer without needing to ask his father. "It was soon after we settled here, in 1997."

After the siege. After the separation. She will ask of course. Anything in the 1990s will bring up the war and foreigners always want to know about the war. Marko doesn't mind. It isn't something they usually talk about. It is the years after the war they discuss. The years when his mother couldn't find work as a pharmacist because she didn't know the right people, didn't belong to the right group. She ended up working in an art gallery, which worked out well for his father. Back then companies, businesses, government offices, they were all run mainly by one group. They were either Croatian or Bosniak. Most of the Serbs had left their city.

"Can I enquire where he was during the war?" the journalist asks softly.

Marko knew it was coming. It had to, of course. Marko expected it. He can recount it easily, but not in detail. The details are not part of either of their words. There isn't a way to translate those. They keep them for themselves, not even sharing them with each other.

"He was in Sarajevo during the siege," says Marko. "We all were."

Marko was eight when the city turned into a warzone, the Serbs firing on them from the hills above, trapping them in the city below. At first, his father tried to go to work. Josip was teaching art at a nearby school. Then the school was struck and there was no need for an art teacher—or a teacher of any kind. Marko's parents spent their days hauling water and food to their fourth-floor apartment, dodging sniper bullets. Outside they stuck to the shadows, walking close to the edge of the apartment buildings hoping they wouldn't be seen. The open spaces were the worst, if they had to cross them, they sprinted. Marko would watch them leave from the window, following them until they were out of sight, not realizing he was holding his breath until he turned away and it escaped from his chest in a long sigh.

Marko was rarely allowed out. He stopped going to school early in the siege. He missed the walk to school, kicking the conkers that fell from the horse chestnut trees in the fall, sweating under his obligatory snowsuit in winter. Now every day was the same. No walks, no teachers, no friends. He told himself he didn't miss his friends, because if he did, he would worry about them and wonder what happened to them when fighting erupted in their neighborhoods.

His parents taught him what they could from books. But they were tired, hungry, and distracted and he learned little. History was particularly challenging. They avoided anything that touched on conflict related to what was happening. European history was out. Instead, Marko learned the names of all the countries in Africa. In his dreams he saw lions and giraffes, pyramids and savannas.

As he approaches a roundabout, Marko notes the modernish building across the way. The journalist notices the pockmarked, roofless building next to it.

"There are still so many destroyed buildings," she says. It is sort of a question.

Marko doesn't notice the ruins anymore. The walls with bullet holes, the houses with missing roofs, trees growing where there was once a kitchen or a bedroom. He notices the palm tree that has grown in the middle of one building. One of his friends lives on the second floor of a building where the first floor is a mess, windows long gone, the insides in total disorder.

"They haven't been repaired because no one agrees on the owner," he says.

He remembers one case. The couple was killed in the fighting. They didn't have children, so the house went to their three nephews. The nephews couldn't decide on what to do with the house, so it stayed as it is, damaged and empty.

"Some of the owners are dead, others are not living here. The homes might be Bosniak in a Croatian part of town or backwards."

"Oh, I understand," she says. But she can't understand, not really.

One day when they were still in Sarajevo Marko snuck out to play soccer with a few other boys in the building. They didn't go far, just a little way away from the apartment entrance where there was a small open space. Marko was just about to kick the ball between the two crumpled cans they were using as goal markers when Jakov screamed. Marko turned around to see the thirteen-year-old boy on the ground. His right leg was twisted at a weird angle, the lower half mushy like ground meat.

"Sniper!" someone shouted.

They all ran toward the building. None of them stopped to help Jakov. Instead, they watched silently from the lobby as Jakov screamed. A man eventually came by and hefted Jakov on his shoulder, carrying him the two flights of stairs to Jakov's apartment, the lift having been out of commission since early in the conflict when they lost electricity.

Later Marko ran into Jakov on the stairway. He was using crutches, the lower half of his right leg no longer there. Marko didn't know what to say. They nodded at each other and then Marko ran down the rest of the stairs. After that whenever Marko heard the thump of the crutches on the stairwell, he would either slow down or hurry up so he would not have to see Jakov and his missing leg. Eventually Jakov was taken to America to be fit with a prosthetic.

Marko doesn't tell any of this to the American journalist.

"They got me out early in the siege," he says. But early is relative, since the siege lasted four years. Marko was smuggled out in the second year, after Jakov was taken to America but before he returned. A former colleague of Josip's had a car and was willing to drive Marko out of the besieged city and beyond the many checkpoints. They made it all the way to Croatia. Marko lived there with his grandparents for three years, wondering the whole time when his parents would join him. If they would join him.

"My mom got out next, and then my dad a while later," he says.

They are at the top of the hill now, by the humongous cross.

"Do you want to get out and see it?" Marko asks.

His father has already opened his door and walked to the edge of the hill where you can look down on the city nestled below. From here it looks quaint, peaceful. A small enclave with an emerald-green river running through it. A river that splits the city between Bosniaks and Croats, between East and West. That happened during the war. From up here it is hard to tell the difference. Only the churches and mosques stand out.

"Is that the old town?" the journalist asks, pointing to the east side of the river.

"Yes, and there is the bridge," Marko says, pointing to a tiny speck that is the reconstructed Ottoman era bridge all the tourists come to see.

Josip wants to know if she has seen the bridge.

"Have you been to Old Town and the bridge?" Marko asks.

"Yes, it is beautiful," she says. "I went to the museum as well, the one on the war."

Marko nods. He has never been there. They built the museum ten years ago. For the tourists.

Marko wants to show her something different. The palm tree. They don't normally grow in this region of Bosnia. The vines and other flora that have overtaken the war damaged buildings make sense. The palm tree growing inside a destroyed structure does not. It is off topic, though, and out of the way. Marko keeps it to himself, unsure how he could work it in to the conversation.

They head back to the car, stopping by the oversize cross on the way. It is too big to capture in a photo, too nondescript to stand by and admire. They simply mark that they have seen it in their memories and move on. As they are settling back into the car Anya calls. Marko puts it on speaker knowing the American won't understand.

"Can you pick up diapers on the way home?" she asks.

"Yes."

"When will you be home?"

"Soon."

He hangs up. He needs his full concentration and both hands to handle the winding roads. His father keeps an eye out for the stations he created as they make their way down the hill. The first one is one of the last, eleven or twelve, Marko misses the number. The image is carved into a flat rock about five feet tall and seven feet wide. The main person in the carving is not Jesus, who is on the ground, but a man with a hammer nailing Jesus to the cross. Neither Jesus nor the man have facial features. They are just outlines.

"Can I get a picture of your father standing by it?" she asks.

Seeing the phone held out like a camera, his father moves closer to the art, to the journalist. He wants them both in the picture and for Marko to take it. Marko has a picture like this at home, only it is him and not a foreign journalist standing next to the carving. The carving is not one of Marko's favorites but it is well known, and he used to carry the photo around as proof of his father's importance, bringing it out to show people as if his father's prominence would keep them from hurting him. It worked, sometimes.

They get back in the car and head down into the Croatian part of the city and the park where Josip's Muhammad Ali statue is. They skip the second station Josip carved. They are all rather similar and the journalist didn't seem interested in seeing another one. Marko was glad to keep moving. Josip was eager to get to his next monument.

They pass through Sycamore Alley, the nickname for a street shaded by large sycamore trees planted in 1888 for a visiting Austro-Hungarian prince. Several of them have outgrown their spots and burst through the roadway. They pass the bars and cafes with their Croatian flags hanging out front in support of the national Croatian football team playing later that day.

"You might want to avoid this street tonight. It could get rowdy," Marko says.

"Thanks, I will," she says. Then she shifts the conversation from football fights to the siege. "During the siege, none of you were injured?"

The war again. Marko thought they had finished with that. When the email arrived talking about monuments and monuments only, Josip and Marko had been pleased. Josip made Marko look at the words over and over again even though they were in Bosnian and he could read them. He couldn't believe she wanted to talk about his work and not the war. He was modest about his art and was surprised someone outside his small country had noticed it.

And now here they are driving around Marko's city looking at all its beauty and talking about everything that was destroyed. Marko always thought the history here, the monuments his father made, were what his son Luka would see. But what if he too sees the bombed-out buildings and the dividing line. Maybe it is better to raise him in a place that has been rebuilt, a place where the conflict is not so recent and raw. A place like Germany.

"My mom was shot by a sniper, but she's okay," he says.

"Where? What happened?" the journalist fires back.

"It was in her hip, when she was fleeing. She left before my dad."

"But she's okay?"

"It bothers her sometimes, she walks with a limp, and it stiffens up on her," he says. "As she gets older it gives her more trouble, but yeah, she's okay."

"That must be hard."

"We were lucky, we all survived."

After they resettled here, Marko heard that Jakov shot himself. Jakov's father was already dead, killed in the fighting. Marko glances at his father sitting beside him, patiently waiting until he translates what is being said. His hair line is receding, but he still has a pretty full head of white hair and a little mustache.

Marko tells his father they are talking about the war. His father nods. "Tell her we are lucky," he says.

"I already did," says Marko.

His father nods again. They are at his modern statue now, the one she really is writing about. She walks all around it, writing down whatever she sees. She points to the inscription at the base.

"What does it say?" she asks.

Marko comes closer, he can't remember the words anymore. One letter is missing but the shadow of where the metal marker was reveals its shape.

"It is a dedication to the city," he says.

Everything his father built is for the city. His home. Where they moved after the war, where his father was born and raised. And yet in the years after the war his father has only voted sporadically. Marko has never voted. It seems pointless when the outcome is already decided. The three different groups—Croats, Serbs and Bosniaks—will rule the country separately, placing their friends in positions of power. Children will keep attending separate schools, not to avoid conflict, but because each side has been given power and no one wants to give it up. Thirty years after the war and they remain divided. His father's generation talks about how they were all one once, under Tito, a dictator. Josip doesn't see him that way, but Marko does. He has no memories of that time. He was too young when it all came crashing down. He doesn't want Luka to live with the uncertainty, always wondering when the fragile peace will combust. It feels like it could. Russia is pressuring the Serbs. The West is building up the Bosniaks.

Marko isn't an artist. He can't build monuments for his son to stand under. What he can do is take him somewhere where there are no reminders of his country's division. Of the weight of what it means to be Croatian in Bosnia. In Germany he can be Luka. And Marko can be his father.

Marko goes back to the car, leaves the two of them to figure things out on their own. They take a selfie, smile and gesture. Marko isn't annoyed with them, just tired. Of all the art his father has produced the Muhammad Ali statue is his most famous and the one Marko likes the least. It stands only three feet tall forcing viewers to come in close to see the detailed muscles on the stomach, the soft lines on the face. Muhammad Ali is standing with his gloves on looking out at the green space in front of him. Marko finds the statue aggressive, as if Muhammad Ali is about to throw a punch.

He calls Anya.

"Where are you?" she asks.

"At the Muhamad Ali monument."

"So, you're still with your father and the journalist?"

"Yes."

"When are you coming home?"

"Soon," he says.

And he means it. He will drop the journalist at her hotel. Then he will drop his father at his apartment. Along the way he will buy diapers and put the baby seat back in the middle of the backseat. Then he will take the elevator to their third-floor apartment. He will walk inside and hug Anya and Luka. Tomorrow, he will tell her about the job offer in Germany—and that he plans to take it.

S.E. Wilson

The Ranch

The radio is off and the windows are down. Teddy drives the speed limit and takes the long way. He's not in much of a hurry. He knows that it has to be done, that the papers will be signed, and the land, the ranch, will no longer be his, be his family's, as it has for over a hundred years, since before the Civil War.

Before he pulls into the parking lot of the Denny's, he can see his cousins' cars parked in front. He parks beside them. He looks into their cars but they're not there. He shuts off the engine and listens to it tick, wishing that he still smoked. He could use a cigarette. He rubs his eyes then heads inside.

They're sitting in a back corner booth. He smiles at a waitress carrying a pot of coffee. If he were wearing a hat, he would've tilted it.

"Sorry I'm late," he says to the table.

Cindy scoots over and Teddy sits beside her. Across from them is Jim, the oldest of the three cousins. His thick hands hide the coffee mug in front of him.

"It's no bother. How are you?" Jim asks.

"I'm good. How are you two?"

"I'm fine. Ready to get this done," Cindy says.

"Have you guys ordered?"

"We were waiting for you," Jim says.

The waitress comes and they order their lunches. Two BLTs and a chicken-fried steak.

"So, you've thought more about the offer?" Jim asks.

"I have. Some."

"Have you thought more about what we talked about?"

Teddy nods.

"I know this is what's best."

"The trees that aren't yet dead are dying. The drought and the sinking water table has dried it all up. It will take hundreds of thousands of dollars to get it producing and profitable again. Not that it ever really was.

At least it hasn't been for decades. And all the equipment is on its last legs. The John Deere too."

Teddy nods again.

"Thirty-five an acre ain't bad. Especially during these times. That's an awful lot of money for us three. Granddad would approve. And your mother and father would approve. It was always a business, and it's time to sell."

"I know."

"This is life changing money, Teddy," Cindy says. "It'll do more than that dusty land and those damn trees."

"Raise your hand if you accept the Crabtree's offer of thirty-five thousand an acre."

Cindy and Jim raise their hands. Teddy doesn't.

"You don't need me to raise my hand. Two is majority."

"But we want you to be okay with this decision," Jim says.

"I've come to terms with it."

"You can finally pay off those medical bills for Sara's treatments," Cindy says. "Since the damn insurance won't."

"It's time, Teddy. Hell, it's been time. We'll sign the papers next Wednesday at the attorney's office."

Teddy sighs and looks across the empty dining room, through the windows, at his old truck in the sun. Maybe this is for the best. But he can't shake a deep feeling that he can't quite describe. A feeling of giving up, of being cut down, of no longer being. Of being alone.

When he gets home he surprises his wife in the kitchen. She jumps a little and places her hand on her flat chest.

"Jesus! You scared me!" Sara says. "What are you doing home early?"

"It's Friday. Just thought I'd get a head start on the weekend."

Teddy grabs a cold beer from the fridge and sits at the kitchen table. Sara leans her back against the counter, the sunlight through the window a halo behind her.

"How was the meeting?"

"Wasn't much of a meeting."

"Well, what did y'all decide on?"

Teddy takes a sip of beer and wipes it from his lips.

"We're selling. Thirty-five an acre."

"Thirty-five thousand?"

"Yeah."

Her eyes widen. She knows that's a lot of money. Life changing money. She moves off the counter and sits across from her husband, putting her hands on his.

"I know this hasn't been easy."

"At least it's done.

"Hungry?"

"Not really, but I'll eat."

"I'll start dinner early then."

She squeezes his hand and gets up.

Teddy takes his beer to the backyard and sits in the sun in a web strap folding chair. He closes his eyes, trying to remember all he can about his time growing up on the ranch. But his memories never do come as fluid scenes, it's always more like flipping through an old photo album. But like the sun on his face, there's a comforting warmth to each and every one of those old photos.

After dinner he and Sara watch TV. They sit on the couch together, but as the clock ticks forward they lean further back and adjust into each other until they lie beside each other, their eyes becoming heavy. Teddy has one arm behind her head, the other over her, his hand resting on her stomach. He never goes much higher. He knows that she knows why, her absent breasts a reminder of what he almost lost.

Sleep is restless and he wakes up early and is still tired. Sara is asleep and she snores. He carefully gets out of bed to not disturb her and takes a leak, then goes to the kitchen to make the coffee. Sitting at the kitchen table he watches the night sky gradually brighten to morning and the house fill with light.

"You're up early," Sara says as she enters the kitchen, tying her robe.

"Did I wake you?"

"No, I smelled the coffee."

She pours herself a cup and tops off Teddy's.

"Thanks."

"Looks like it's going to be a nice day."

"I think I'm going to go out to the ranch."
"Would you like for me to come?"
"I think I'd prefer to go alone."

She sits on his lap, almost spilling his hot coffee, and wraps her arms around him, resting her head on his.

"Be careful," she says.

The ranch is an hour drive west on country roads past rice fields and almond orchards. The white blossoms blow in the breeze like a spring snow, but the blue sky is cloudless and dotted with dark birds. Teddy could drive these old roads with his eyes closed, he knows them as if they ran through his own body. He likes to think that his great, great grandparents took their wagons along the dirt that's below the asphalt when they settled in this county all those years ago, decades before the turn of the twentieth century. Everything here is a tendril connecting him to his past, to his family.

As he crosses the bridge he slows down and looks out into the orchards, at the oldest walnut trees on their land that are still alive, planted nearly fifty years ago, before he was even born, by his father and uncle. His mother helped whitewash the trees. He's seen proof of their happiness in old photos. Their black and white smiles brighter than the day was hot. Past the old trees is empty land, full of weeds and trunks, where the trees died and had to be taken out. He turns down a gravel road that leads to the house built by his great grandfather, where his father was born, where he grew up after life had taken his parents, a house that's now nothing more than a skeleton of what it once was. The windows are broken, the roof rotten, weeds and vines overtake the wood siding and porch, the brick chimney burnt and broken after being hit by lightning three years ago.

He parks his truck beside his grandfather's rusted '54 Chevy, beneath the twisted oak near the barn. The barn doors are shut and locked and he realizes that he forgot the key. But he didn't come here to see the John Deere, the broken-down harvester, or the old tools and miscellaneous junk. He came for the land and the trees, even for the crumbling house where he grew into a man. He sits for a moment, then opens the truck door and gets out, his boots stomping into the dust below him.

He inhales deeply, the smell of dirt and spring filling his chest. He walks around the house, too cautious to step onto the rotten porch. No one has been inside for years. But his memory will forever see it as it always was. He sees his grandmother at the kitchen table drinking coffee and looking out the back screen door, watching the men tend the orchards. After a day's work, his grandfather sipping whiskey and smoking cigarettes on the porch, listening to the crickets. Upstairs was his bedroom, where he'd lost his virginity thirty years ago when his grandparents were celebrating their anniversary in Reno, and where he learned that his grandfather had died from a stroke. He had been lying in bed, reading a Sports Illustrated with Jack Nicklaus on the cover—Master of Them All. Two years later his grandmother passed away. He was eighteen then, and he'd moved out on his own. Barn swallows erupt from a second story window and startle him, and further remind him of how nothing can ever stay the same and that everything will eventually decay and make room for something new.

The orchards are thick with weeds and broken branches, different from how they had always been before. Now quiet and desolate, the springs and summers before were bustling and full of life. The space between the rows of trees once clean packed and weeded ground, now barely passable. As he moves inward, cautious of snakes, he forges his own path through the grove of trees that he helped plant twenty years ago, the trees all dead or dying now, the holes not dug wide enough. The oldest trees are the only ones that remain, and he knows that they will be uprooted and something new will grow in their place. He likes the old trees. He likes knowing that his father and mother planted them, he likes knowing that they're alive, that the deep roots still provide nourishment. Even if the trees don't produce like they once did, they are alive. He sits on the ground, his back against one of these trees, in the shade, above the roots, and he closes his eyes.

A dog barks and Teddy's eyes open. Through the trees, about fifty yards away, is a tan skinny dog. Teddy scoots his back up against the tree and stands. He looks around and sees no one. He listens and hears no one. There's nothing but the birds. He takes a step toward the dog and the dog seems skittish, so he stops and kneels. He stares at the dog and the dog stares back. Its eyes are big and brown.

Teddy tries calling the dog, putting his hand out, but the dog doesn't come. It turns and scurries away. Teddy watches it disappear into the orchard, then turns and begins walking back to the truck. But less than halfway back, he hears something behind him and turns to see the dog. The dog stops. Teddy looks around, but still doesn't see another soul. Only trees.

"Where did you come from?" Teddy asks the dog.

He continues walking, looking back every fifty yards or so to see the dog still following. Back at the tuck, the dog stays at the edge of the orchard, between the trees. Teddy drops his tailgate and sits. The dog sits too. They stay like that for some time, staring at each other, or Teddy looking at the changing sky through the trees. It's warm and humid and Teddy is glad to be in the shade of the oak. The dog stands and moves closer and sits again. Teddy sees that it's a male and wishes he had some food for him in his truck, something to coax him nearer. He looks hungry.

His grandfather's truck is closer to the dog, so Teddy lifts himself and goes to his grandfather's Chevy, lowering the tailgate and sitting there. He's not as shaded as before, but the intermittent sunlight through the branches feels good. It's only after a moment that the dog stands and closes the distance between the two. As it gets closer, Teddy can see the bald patches and scars where hair no longer grows. He lowers himself onto the dusty ground. He puts his hands out. The dog gets nearer and nearer, until he's within reach. Teddy reaches for him, gently touching the dog's neck. His coat is coarse, and it smells. But he allows Teddy to touch him. He moves forward, almost leaning into Teddy's hand, looking into Teddy's eyes.

"I wonder what Sara would think," Teddy says aloud.

He scratches the dog behind the ear. The dog pants and Teddy realizes that he must be thirsty. He grabs his coffee mug from the truck and fills it with water from the hose near the barn. He places it in front of the dog. The dog hesitates, smelling at the mug, but then drinks from it.

Teddy tilts the mug, water spilling from it, water spilling from the dog's mouth. Teddy refills the mug three more times. The dog lies at his feet. He already looks better, his eyes brighter. Despite the malnutrition and the mange, Teddy sees something good. He bends down to get closer.

"You look like a George. That was my great grandfather's name."

Teddy drives with the windows down, the wind whipping in and out, around him and the dog—around him and George. He pushes his foot against the gas, the sun setting behind them, the daylight burning away above the ranch. And although he still feels the ache of unachievable yearning, he feels better than he has for some time, and he turns up the radio.

Stephen D. Abney

Frog Bottoms: Hannah's Birthday

We lived in the marshy land near where Little South River enters South River, near the shuttered lumber mills and the homes of other mill workers, in the section of town known as Frog Bottoms. No one of any importance ever came from there, not even a city councilman.

I'm one of those not-important people. I was born there on December seventh, 1926.

South River floods most years, so our house was built up on cinderblocks. We managed. Daddy went in his boat to fetch groceries, mainly milk and bread. A slough ran behind Main Street, and when the river was high, he'd tie up behind the grocery.

The '37 flood was different. Water reached the second story of the courthouse. Daddy figured the river was thirty-five feet above normal. They painted a white line on the bricks to show how high it was, in case we forgot.

Otherwise, my life was normal. It was the Great Depression, of course, but when you've lived like that long enough, it becomes like every other day. I didn't know a time before that.

Once, I was at the pharmacy on Main, thumbing through magazines while Momma picked up some things. They'd let you look if you didn't overdo it. The almanac had a section on what had happened each day. Not much ever happened on my birthday—some famous people died, some were born—except it was the day in 1917 when the United States joined the Great War, the war that Daddy fought in.

My fifteenth birthday was the second Sunday of Advent, the one when they light the purple Peace candle. That morning, Momma and I walked to church while Daddy and my brothers went hunting. They left before we did that morning, put on hip waders so they could crisscross Little South. By the time we returned from church, they had skinned and gutted six gray squirrels.

Momma cut the legs off and put the backs and livers in a bowl of water in the icebox. Later, she'd boil them to get the meat off so we could have squirrel soup with greens another day. For lunch, she dredged the legs in eggs, milk, and flour with salt and pepper, and fried them to a chestnut crisp. She opened a Mason jar of green beans to heat up and set out biscuits left from breakfast.

Squirrel is a lean, stringy meat. I had to be careful eating it since there were always shotgun pellets to avoid. Chomp down on one of those and you'll know it.

That afternoon while Daddy and my brothers were cleaning their shotguns on the stoop, his cousin, Tommy Clifton, walked past. He said we should turn on the radio.

Daddy cursed when he heard the news. Not one of those words that you say if you smash your thumb. This was full-on, Ten-Commandments, Lord's-name-in-vain, go-straight-to-hell cursing. Words I can't repeat.

Momma gave him the stink eye. "George! The children."

He cursed again. He damned the Japanese and the Germans, but especially Woodrow Wilson.

I went to him. "Daddy, what's wrong?"

"I'm sorry, Pumpkin. When I went to the Great War, they told me it was the war to end all wars. Wilson promised, that lying sonofa—"

"George, please," Momma said.

"Thompson, Smitty, Kowalski, Washington, Beantown, the rest—my whole squad shot at, some wounded, some dead. For what? If that wasn't the war to end all wars, what the hell was it for? Damn the politicians. Damn them all." Of course, he didn't just say "damn."

Then I saw him mist up, which he did on those rare occasions when he talked about his war buddies. It wasn't crying, but if you knew what to look for, you could tell. He took a breath, wiped the back of his fist across his nose, and set his jaw.

"You know they'll come after Eddie right away," he said, "since he's nineteen."

"I know," Momma said.

"Pray it's over soon," he said. "Harold's a senior. They'll be after him soon as he graduates."

"Maybe it'll be quick, like the Great War," Eddie said. "We weren't there even a year."

"Maybe," Daddy said, "but I doubt it. Get the maps."

Harold went into the boys' room and came back with their prized world atlas. "There's Hawaii, The Philippines, and Japan," he said, pointing to them one at a time. "They're a long ways from Kentucky."

"France was a far piece too," Daddy said. "Didn't matter."

Cornerstone

poetry by writers K–12

Erika Prasthofer

Poetic Reserve

Admirable poetry is vulnerable,
smooth with the vulnerable subject
like aloe vera chop, sesame seed
sprinkle of a sin, slender curve
of narcissus stem. This way, expression
may proliferate and linger like ivy, and yet
the style is never going to get to me;
the style is never going to get to me
(because) it's inevitable that it must.
My poetry is peel-crusted, dry peel, zest
not-yet grated, too thin
to be grated for fresh garnish.
Tonight, I feel Hemingway-succinct,
but my message is fettered
by chimeras, deliberate enigma,
that turmeric hem of a tulip, rim
around the biological wine glass.
I hear the ringing, too, finger slick
with rouge, with a less ephemeral zest
I still don't dare to taste, (eternally)
revolving.

Jack DeBoyace

Deterioration, They Said

Séance in a forever tempo, the
  hawk glides mistaken for a god only
in the allure of transgression. My Hun-
  ter Biden fugue kind of blue, oh, tonight
I'm tangled in your headlights. Car crashes
  aren't like the movies: the music's still
on, "Teenage Dream" caught in a futurist
  aphasia. Voice a-jest suspended by
a drawn-out falsetto as prayer, mix-
  ture of rapture and diseased cheer and we
fall in love on purpose. Haunted iris,
  I saw you across the room among mem-
orial sludge in flux, a ringing noise:
  Deneb, de-neb. Yes, I'm a believer

Jack DeBoyace

Valley

Cue hips against staccato
them woo bodies tempest
trill again I am a bird now
as you make me sea
                    each of the waves
an eye once, though
sexy Rorschach test
no structure immune from memory
they think it's a conspiracy
                    dolly zoom
the images of last night's wreck
  we'll leave it alone   when I slick back this elegy   pompadour-ish
O Miley   my witness
  I wanted to be a pop star   my grandma convinced I was possessed by
Satan   dancing to "We Can't Stop" worshipping
                                  and queer
                                  and died
                                  and you can only kill me
                                  once.

Pharaoh Jones

Manicured Forest

The manicured forest is a sight to see
Fresh with wigged leaves
Each sold separately
Selling the land as a brand
Is something of a cliche
Found in the way a Bluejay poses
In front of the chromatic lens
Braying to assert dominance
Leaving a plume of a feather
As a business card
With an all new avian font

Colonial bees invade as they do
Sitting on the porch of a native hive
Stingers at the ready, rope in hand
Bracing to give it to the punk
Who won't sell any of their honey

A Tattered Winged Heron glides above the trees
An all new species
Thanks to the hereditary use
Of radioactive pomade
As it flies unstably
It wonders what the hawk ever did
As the hawk approaches on the same flight path
Bruised and battered, cracked beak
He got the hurt put on him
After telling a group of Robins
They didn't need to put that makeup on

Pharaoh Jones

Cabbage and Cantaloupe

I roost up in the hayloft
Heated by the big screen TV
My sisters coo and snore
I ruffle my feathers
Craning my neck downward
And into the tales I have in store

I hail from the searing ground
Where we lived among bears
That hissed and spat
Whilst whipping their ratty tails

If you didn't already know
Chickens are courageous creatures
We mock our predators
With purring trills of resilience

I heard somewhere that humans think we're flightless birds
That's only a lie, spun to make us seem weak
I could scale a tree if I wanted
Even if we were flightless
We sure as cluck ain't fightless

Our talons are undoubtedly lethal
Ripping away at the annelids
We scoured ripe soil for
Plucking away at some greens
And sharpening our poignant beaks on a log

We are not mere "livestock"
If royalty were still a thing
I'd be an earl of the yard
A few of my kind are even so brave
As to roam with a naked presence
Flaunting supple skin to the Theropods in the sky

Of course, there has been casualties
Feathery-foot men on the battlefield
Losing lives to rabid teeth and claws

While their body feeds the gangrenous filth
The warrior soul crosses the river Chicx
And enters Fowlhalla
Where one may groom thyself thoroughly
Before bathing in a divot of dust

These tales may be quite bleak
But understand . . . the world has it out for us
Even so
My sisters sleep peacefully

Adebola Adenle

Interphase

—After "the mother" by Gwendolyn Brooks

I am sorry. If
when we were being separated, I
forgot what I really meant to say. My sy-stole,
potassium pump and the thunder's rumble sent your
bird's nests and flying swallow births
out of town. The vespers of dirt and
shrine bells are the only way your
kin could reach me with all the names.

Jovina Zion Pradeep

Caramelized Marble

Jade scalloped lace aligns waves of turquoise,
Frozen coral blooms immortalized in sand dollars

Blown ashore. Spongy trees embellished with sparkling
Rubies, haven of footprints gone rock climbing.

Golden sequin threads, spun seashell ashes adorning
Foamy sky. Chimney of fiery dewdrops echoing

In waterfall of coconut ambrosia dripping from
Branches, extending into sunset above as hues of twilight

Reflect onto window wipers. Sandy railways on tracks
uncharted lead to relics on teak: circles of age as evolution

Stretches balloons once never blown into scanty clouds
Sailing across an abyss of darkness. Thrifted scarves graze

Shore's shoulder as sand dunes become the hills of a fertile
valley, a grassy womb open with inspiration. Fawns nuzzle

Where a waterfall of daisies falls. The yellow sunny dandelion
Lingers in wait as flying lanterns arrive from their hiding places.

Fishes dressed in horseshoes of frozen blood, gills of high-heeled
shoes. Leather scales and cowboy saddles on shiny scales.

Jellyfish tripods dangle in mid-floatation as strings of sunlight
Vaporize, vibrated echoes encompass emerald leaves of seaweed.

Edible capillaries of syrup salt coated in crystalline attire,
Smoke twirling through crevices of hewn rock. Rumbling roar

Of white noise on shore as venous bristles of earth twirl in
Cacophony of wind, tousling bubbly trees with broccoli heads.

Sophie Watson

Resentment

I pull gravity around me
with the growing claws of my rage.
My anger is catastrophic,

hurricaning in the jar of my skull.
Lightning cracks veins through the glass.
It fractures, expands.

The air is sucked from the space.
I am taking it all, asphyxiating
everyone around me with this silence.

Warping the light with the enormity
of my resentment, the leach of sunshine,
the swallow of houses and cars

into the dark mouth of my enmity.
It is palpable, this feeling, the heavy
crush of the elephant's foot.

In the room there are my things
once stolen: the aerosols, the sharps,
the music and the windows.

In the closet there are the bones
of my suffering, the human I used to be,
stripped into sequences of memory.

I am out of it now, but I am left
trying to purge the stains of its blood

from my hands, the time I spent

in the soaked soil of a gravesite.
In the shadow of a hospital,
I crush the armband, I keep the fear

somewhere easy to access.
Tap the marrow of this distress,
lick it clean, gnaw, and smile.

Sophie Watson

Amy

Jumbled nonsense, we talk in the halls
past midnight in the black hour.
Your voice rambles, a shallow creek
or the pitter-patter of some small animal.
But you are not some small animal, Amy.
You are not anyone's mother.
You should not spend time in raw-handed,
bubble-making, dish-washing, scrubbing
skin to the bone. I do not comprehend
the Spanish-stained accent, the hushed tone
of the stories you tell me about family and home.
Yet I will listen. The minutes fall, softening,
as attendants usher me away to an Ativan heaven.
You're still here fighting the devil in you,
just asking them to play a happy song.
But your favorite song is "Set Fire to the Rain,"
and we share a birthday, and you were here
the last time I was too haunted to stand.
Now, I savor this moment, I understand.
In a dream pieced together from your words,
I see you released, running in the dark alone,
wanting the cool blackness to consume you.
Your favorite color is black.

Clara Deckker

Iron Oxide

I pick at my split-ends,
even if they're not broken,
the loves I had spun from golden
into dust.
You sit next to me,
watch as I bend over debris, the shiny cars I watered
into rust.

You lift my head,
chin in the palm of your hands,
remove the remaining strands
from my grasp.
I watch as they fall,
slipping into the tattered vault
where my infatuations go
to fast.

Eva Alcaraz-Monje

Appalachia is Contagious

I've begun to light cigarettes at noon,
watching the smoke bend across
conifers that reek of corn syrup.

I "bless your heart"
to those I do not love
because they know
I don't.

My neck bears a cross
that I don't believe in,
tarnished iron with a simple remember-
ance of God and someone
with Him.

I drink Ale 8 like honey nectar,
sugar caking the gas station
t-shirt I found on the rack
for spare change.

A knife is secured in my back pocket
with loose denim thread and an urge
to flick it open like swings
on a midnight playground.

I drive on roads that don't want
to be paved, bumping
some heathen music alongside
the cows and the horses and
the buzzards.

My soul aches
for coleslaw and grits and potato salad
because this is "y'all are family" love,
and I am tired of denying it.

Contributors' Notes

Stephen D. Abney, a graduate of the University of Kentucky, comes from a line of Kentuckians that reaches back to before statehood. His published work includes articles in US Department of Defense publications, creative nonfiction in *The Writing Disorder*, and a poem he sold to *Rattle*. During the Covid shutdown, he completed a Michigan State course in novel writing.

Virginia Lee Alcott is a self-taught artist and a Kentucky licensed professional art therapist (LPAT). She has exhibited her art statewide. Her current interest is in photography aligned with poetry, and capturing images that reflect justice and equity. Virginia tries to capture images in her poetry that relate nature to healing, justice, and relationships. She loves listening to, reading, and writing poetry.

Grace Bauer has published six books of poems—most recently *Unholy Heart: New and Selected Poems* (Backwaters Press). She also co-edited the anthology *Nasty Women Poets: An Unapologetic Anthology of Subversive Verse.* Her poems, essays, stories, and reviews have appeared in numerous anthologies and journals. After living and teaching in Lincoln, Nebraska, for more than twenty-five years, she has recently returned to her native Pennsylvania. She lives and writes in Philadelphia.

A Fulbright fellow (Albania, 2011) and Pushcart nominee, **Gregory Byrd** has published poetry and prose in *South Florida Poetry Journal, Puerto del Sol, Tampa Review, Willow Springs,* and *Baltimore Review.* Greg's poetry chapbook, *The Name of the God Who Speaks,* won the Robert Phillips Prize from Texas Review Press. Greg graduated from the writing workshops at Eckerd College and Florida State University and teaches writing and literature at St. Petersburg College in Tarpon Springs, Florida. www.gregorybyrd.org

Abigail Byrd-Stapleton is a poet and artist from Paintsville, Kentucky, located in the divine Kentucky Wildlands. She earned her MFA in creative writing from the Bluegrass Writers Studio in 2022, and is currently a migratory writer, living in Germany with her partner and their two dogs. When she's not devouring poetry (figuratively) and loaded tater tots (literally), she's probably trying to get lost and go mad with ancient wisdom in the forest. She hopes you have a pleasant day.

Nan Byrne is the author of two books. Her latest poetry chapbook, *Wonder City*, is from Plan B Press. Her work has appeared in *Michigan Quarterly Review, Seattle Review, New Orleans Review, Texas Poetry Review, Potomac Review, Phoebe,* and *Cherry Tree,* and is forthcoming in *Union Springs* and *Willow.* She is the associate fiction editor at *Maine Review* and is currently at work on a novel.

Tiffany Calvert's paintings incorporate diverse technologies, including fresco, 3D modeling, and data manipulation. John Yau, in his *Hyperallergic* profile, compares their "improvisational riffs and fractured views" to de Kooning. Calvert's work has been exhibited at the Lawrimore Project (Seattle, Washington), E.TAY Gallery (New York), the Speed Museum (Louisville, Kentucky), the Susquehanna Art Museum (Pennsylvania), and Cadogan Contemporary (London), among others. Residencies include the Djerassi Resident Artists Program, I-Park, and ArtOmi International Arts Center, where she received a Geraldine R. Dodge Fellowship. Calvert has received grants from the Great Meadows Foundation and the Pollock-Krasner Foundation. She is Associate Professor and MFA Director at the Sam Fox School of Design + Visual Arts at Washington University in St. Louis.

Willie Carver Jr. is a minoritized youth advocate, Kentucky Teacher of the Year, and the author of *Gay Poems for Red States*, a Stonewall, American Library Association, Read Appalachia, Whippoorwill, and Book Riot-award winning collection currently shortlisted for the 2024 Judy Gaines Young Book Award. His fragmented novel, *Tore All to Pieces,* will be published in Spring 2026 by the University Press of Kentucky. He writes poetry and fiction from Appalachia. Willie believes everyone deserves to feel that they matter.

Katya Cengel has published short stories and essays in *Discretionary Love, Zaum, Literary Hub, The Rumpus*, and *River Teeth*. Her features have been in *New York Times Magazine* and *Smithsonian Magazine*, among others. Cengel is the author of four books including Independent Publisher Book Awards-winner *Straitjackets and Lunch Money* and *From Chernobyl with Love*.

Thomas Dukes has published a prize-winning poetry collection, *Baptist Confidential,* and his second collection, *Gospels From the Lower Shelf,* appeared in 2023. He has published a number of poems, short fiction, nonfiction, journalism, scholarship, etc. He lives in Richfield, Ohio, with his husband, two cats, and a dog.

Avra Elliott is a queer writer of Scottish and Mexican heritage from New Mexico. A graduate of the MFA Program for Writers at Warren Wilson College, Elliott's fiction has been published in *Waxwing, Sweet Tree Review, Shadowgraph Quarterly, Contrary,* and *Noctua Review,* where her work was runner-up for the Neo Americana Fiction Contest. Elliott's poetry has appeared in several journals including *Barrow Street, Crab Orchard Review, Tinderbox, Tupelo Quarterly, Comstock Review, Southword,* and *Fairy Tale Review*. Her chapbook, *Desert Selkie,* was a semifinalist for the 2018 Sunken Garden Poetry Chapbook Award from Tupelo Press.

Emilio Gomez is a second-generation Cuban born and raised in South Florida. Growing up in an environment surrounded by drugs, violence, and ignorance, Emilio turned to words at a young age in an attempt to understand himself and the world around him. In his writing, he tries to capture the emotional impressions that he and others often feel but struggle to articulate. Emilio currently lives in Stuart, Florida, with his wife, two sons, and silky terrier. Previous prose and poetry have been published in *California Quarterly*, *Door = Jar*, *The Sigma Tau Delta Rectangle*, and *Living Waters Review*. He also publishes on Instagram under the handle salem_vows.

Kelly Granito is a poet and public education researcher who is increasingly inspired by the internal experiences of parenting and domestic life. She lives in Ann Arbor with her husband, kids, cats, and too many plants. Her poetry has been featured in *Iron Horse Review* (forthcoming), *Burrow Press*, *Midwestern Gothic*, *Santa Clara Review*, *3288 Review*, *Noctua Review*, *The Laureate*, and elsewhere.

Alex Green is the author of the poetry collection *Emergency Anthems* (Brooklyn Arts Press) and five novels, including *The Heart Goes Boom* and *The Adventure Teen All-Stars*. He's the editor of *Stereo Embers Magazine* and the host of the Stereo Embers podcast. Alex currently teaches in the English department at Saint Mary's College of California.

Camille Hernandez is the city of Anaheim's third Poet Laureate (2024–2026). She is a Black and Filipina author moving through the world as a *kapwa* womanist. Equipped by her matriarchal cultures and motherhood journey, Camille writes and leads from the fluid depths of tenderness, protection, and intuition. Camille was an inaugural fellow of Roots.Wounds.Words. Storytellers of Color Retreat and a current fellow of The Watering Hole. She authored the biomythography book *The Hero and the Whore*. Her poems are published in *So to Speak*, *Braving the Body*, and *Health Promotion Practice*. She's the editor of *Anaheim Poetry Review*.

Ron Hickerson works in higher education where he helps students navigate the murky waters of academia. When he's not in his office, you can find him wandering around campus, looking for the oldest trees. His previous work has appeared in *The Clayjar Review*, *Solid Food Press*, and *Griffel*.

Lennie Hay is a 2019 MFA graduate in poetry from Spalding University. She grew up between two cultures—Chinese immigrants and Ukrainian German farmers. Born in the Midwest, Lennie currently lives in Southern Indiana next to the Ohio River and in Florida on the Gulf of Mexico. The inspiration from water figures in her poetry. Music, particularly classical and jazz, are central to her life and her poetry. A former public school educator and consultant, Lennie's poetry has been published in national and international print and online journals and in two anthologies. Her book, *Lost in America*, was published in June 2024 by Broadstone Books.

Marcia L. Hurlow is professor emeritus of creative writing, journalism, and TESOL at Asbury University. Her seventh collection of poetry, *Dog Physics*, will be published this fall by The Main Street Rag. She has won the Al Smith Fellowship in Poetry twice and serves as co-editor of *Kansas City Voices*.

Clare Kramer is a junior anthropology major and psychology and creative writing double-minor at Bellarmine University. She grew up on a farm in Southern Indiana and enjoys hearing and telling stories, making art and music, writing, and spending time in nature. Her writing focuses on identity, heritage, and relationship with the natural world.

Kara Lewis is a poet and editor based in Minneapolis and Kansas City. Her poems have appeared or are forthcoming in *The Pinch, Sugar House Review, Paranoid Tree, SWWIM, Rogue Agent, Permafrost*, and elsewhere. Her work has also been featured in the anthology *Stained: an anthology of writing about menstruation*, published by Querencia Press. She is a Best of the Net nominee. You can follow her and her writing on Instagram @kararaylew.

Angie Macri is the author of *Sunset Cue* (Bordighera), winner of the Lauria/Frasca Poetry Prize, and *Underwater Panther* (Southeast Missouri State University Press), winner of the Cowles Poetry Book Prize. An Arkansas Arts Council fellow, she lives in Hot Springs.

Mark Madigan is the author of a chapbook, *Thump and other poems*, published by Finishing Line Press. He holds an MFA from the Naslund-Mann Graduate School of Writing at Spalding University.

Ilan Mochari is the author of the novel *Zinsky the Obscure*. His poetry and fiction have been widely published, appearing in *McSweeney's Quarterly Concern, Salamander, Hobart, J Journal, Juked, Valparaiso Fiction Review, North Dakota Review*, and elsewhere. His work has been nominated for multiple Pushcart Prizes, as well as the Derringer Award, and he is the recipient of a Literature Artist Fellowship grant from the Somerville Arts Council.

Jesse Mountjoy is a native of Horse Cave, Kentucky, and a 1965 graduate of Centre College in Danville, Kentucky. He obtained his law degree in 1969 from Vanderbilt University. He was admitted to practice in Kentucky in 1970 and served a four-year stint as senior trial attorney for the Internal Revenue Service, Regional Counsel's Office, Cincinnati, Ohio, where he tried cases in the U.S. Tax Court. After working with the Internal Revenue Service, Mountjoy moved to Owensboro, Kentucky, in 1974, where he has practiced tax, estate, and trust law in Western Kentucky with the same firm (now Sullivan Mountjoy, PSC) for fifty years. Mountjoy's poetry has appeared in *Open 24 Hours, Wind Magazine, The Sow's Ear Poetry Review, Kentucky Poetry Review, Approaches, Adena, The Small Pond Magazine of Literature, Legal Studies Forum, Southern Indiana Review, Flint Hills Review, Blue Moon Literary and Art Review, The Journal of Kentucky Studies, Exquisite Corpse,* and *Gray's Sporting Journal.* Mountjoy claims a fondness for Flaubert's assertion that "Every lawyer carries within himself the debris of a poet."

Dana Murphy lives in her home state of California. Her poetry and short fiction appear or are forthcoming in *carte blanche magazine, The 2River View, Up the Staircase Quarterly, Obsidian: Literature & Arts in the African Diaspora, Fourteen Hills: The SFSU Review,* and others. In 2024–25, she is a fellow at the Stanford Humanities Center.

Pat Owen is the author of three volumes of poetry: *Crossing the Sky Bridge, Orion's Belt at the End of the Drive,* and *Bardo of Becoming.* A fourth collection is forthcoming from Shadelandhouse Modern Press. Her work has appeared in *Hong Kong Review, Gulf Stream Magazine, The Louisville Review, Raven's Perch,* and *Highland Park Poetry,* as well as in numerous anthologies. She was an award-winner in the Chautauqua Literary Arts Contest. Most recently she was selected as a Finalist in the Atlanta Review International Poetry Competition, and her poem "1974 Sanibel Island" will be published in the Fall 2024 *Atlanta Review.*

Madari Pendas is a Cuban-American writer and artist. She received her MFA from Florida International University, where she was a Lawrence Sanders Fellow, and won the 2021 Academy of American Poets Prize, judged by Major Jackson. Her work has appeared in *Craft, Smokelong Quarterly, The Masters Review, Oyster River Pages, PANK,* and more. She is the author of *Crossing the Hyphen* (2021) and *She Loves me, She Loves me Not* (2025).

Karl Plank is the author of *The Grace of Falling Things* (Grayson Books, forthcoming) and the critical volume *The Fact of the Cage: Reading and Redemption in David Foster Wallace's Infinite Jest* (Routledge, 2021). His poetry has appeared in publications such as *Beloit Poetry Journal, Zone 3,* and *Tahoma Literary Review,* and has been featured on *Poetry Daily.* A native of Louisville, he is the J. W. Cannon Professor of Religion, Emeritus, at Davidson College.

Lizzy Ke Polishan's recent poems appear in *Gulf Coast*, *The Greensboro Review*, *Gigantic Sequins*, *The Notre Dame Review*, *The Banshee*, *RHINO*, and *The Penn Review*, among many others. She is the author of the poetry collection *A Little Book of Blooms* (2020), a poetry reader for *Psaltery & Lyre,* and a guest editor at *Palette*. She lives in Pennsylvania with her husband.

Christy Prahl is an Illinois Arts Council grant recipient and the author of the poetry collections *We Are Reckless* (Cornerstone Press, 2023) and *Catalog of Labors* (Unsolicited Press, forthcoming 2026). A Best of the Net and three-time Pushcart Prize nominee, her work has been featured in *Poetry Daily* as well as many national and international journals, including *CALYX, Sugar House Review*, the *Penn Review*, *Salt Hill Journal*, and others. She has held residencies at Ragdale and the Writers' Colony at Dairy Hollow and splits her time between Chicago and rural Michigan. More of her work can be found at christyprahl.wixsite.com/christy-prahl.

Born in Eastern Washington and raised in Southern California, **E. Reid** has lived and worked in North Alabama and Southern Middle Tennessee since 1998. She and her partner live in an old wood home with a menagerie of critters surrounded by green hills. An alumna of the Naslund-Mann Graduate School of Writing in Louisville, Kentucky, E. Reid also writes poetry and creative nonfiction.

Margaret Rozga, UWM at Waukesha Professor of English Emerita, served as the 2019-2020 Wisconsin Poet Laureate and the 2021 inaugural artist/scholar in residence at the UW Milwaukee at Waukesha Field Station. Her first book, *200 Nights and One Day,* tells the story of Milwaukee's open housing marches in which she was a participant. Her recent books include *Holding My Selves Together: New & Selected Poems* (2021) and *Restoring Prairie* (2024), both published by Cornerstone Press.

Robert Sachs' fiction has appeared in *The Louisville Review*, *Chicago Quarterly Review*, *Free State Review*, *Great Ape*, and *Delmarva Review*, among many others. He holds an MFA in Creative Writing from Spalding University. His story "Vondelpark" was nominated for a Pushcart Prize in 2017, and his story "Old Times" was the fiction winner in the 2021 Tiferet Writing Contest. More of his published stories can be found at bobsachs.weebly.com.

Mary Ellen Talley's poems have been published in journals including *Gyroscope*, *Deep Wild*, and *Banshee*, as well as in several anthologies. Her poems have received three Pushcart nominations. She has three chapbooks: *Postcards from the Lilac City* from Finishing Line Press, *Taking Leave* from Kelsay Press, and *Infusion*, online at *Red Wolf Journal*. Her website is maryellentalley.com.

Poet and essayist **Jeanie Thompson** is the author of *The Myth of Water: Poems from the Life of Helen Keller*, *The Seasons Bear Us*, *White for Harvest: New and Selected Poems*, *Witness*, and *How to Enter the River*. Her poetry and essays on the writing life have been published in *Old Enough: Southern Women Writers and Artists on Creativity and Aging*, *Tributaries*, *Creativity and Compassion*, *Whatever Remembers Us*, *High Horse*, *Working the Dirt*, *All Out of Faith*, *The Best of Crazyhorse*, and *The Southern Poetry Anthology, Volume X: Alabama*.

In 2023 Jeanie retired as Executive Director *Emerita* of the Alabama Writers' Forum, and in June of that year she received the Albert B. Head Legacy Award from the Alabama State Council on the Arts for her work as a literary arts advocate and award-winning poet. Jeanie has been a poetry faculty member of Spalding University's Naslund-Mann Graduate School of Writing since 2002. She lives in Montgomery, Alabama.

Caris Uşoară is a queer, disabled artist, scholar, and emerging poet. She rests on and creates from ancestral, traditional, and contemporary Dakota homelands (Dakota County, Minnesota). Read her poetry forthcoming in *BarBar*.

Whitney Vale is seventy years old and is the recipient of an MFA in Creative Nonfiction from Ashland University. Credits include poetry in *Crab Creek Review*, *Thimble Literary Review*, *RockPaperPoem*, *Rogue Agent*, and *Anti-Heroin Chic*. Prose credits include *Literary Angels*, *Entropy*, *The Rumpus*, and *The Black Fork Review*. Her work is also included in *Awakenings: Stories of Body & Consciousness*, edited by Diane Gottlieb.

Julie Marie Wade writes and publishes poetry, prose, and hybrid forms. Her most recent and forthcoming collections include *The Mary Years* (Texas Review Press, 2024), selected by Michael Martone for the 2023 Clay Reynolds Novella Prize, *Quick Change Artist: Poems* (Anhinga Press, 2025), selected by Octavio Quintanilla for the 2023 Anhinga Prize in Poetry, and *The Latest: 20 Ghazals for 2020* (Harbor Editions, 2025), co-authored with Denise Duhamel. A finalist for the National Poetry Series and a winner of the Lambda Literary Award for Lesbian Memoir, Wade teaches in the creative writing program at Florida International University in Miami and makes her home with Angie Griffin and their two cats in Dania Beach.

Pamela Wax is the author of *Walking the Labyrinth* (Main Street Rag, 2022) and *Starter Mothers* (Finishing Line Press, 2023). Her poems have received two Best of the Net nominations and awards from *Crosswinds*, *Paterson Literary Review*, *Poets' Billow*, *Oberon*, and the Robinson Jeffers Tor House. Other publications include *Barrow Street*, *Tupelo Quarterly*, *The Massachusetts Review*, *Chautauqua*, *The MacGuffin*, *Nimrod*,

Solstice, *Mudfish*, *Connecticut River Review*, *Valparaiso Poetry Review*, and *Slippery Elm*. An ordained rabbi, Pam offers spirituality and poetry workshops online and around the country. She lives in the northern Berkshires of Massachusetts.

Eric Weil lives in Raleigh, North Carolina. Journals ranging from *American Scholar* to *Poetry*, from *Dead Mule* to *Sow's Ear*, and from *Main Street Rag* to *Red Planet* have published his poetry. He has three chapbooks in print.

Ellen Wright is author of the poetry collection *Family Portrait with Oilwell* (2023, Kelsay Books) and the chapbook *In Transit* (2007, Main Street Rag). She has recent work in *Paterson Literary Review*, *Speckled Trout Review*, *Common Ground Review*, and *The Fourth River*, among others.

S. E. Wilson lives in North Carolina with his wife, son, dogs, and cat. His work has appeared or is forthcoming in *Chiron Review*, *Streetlight Magazine*, and *New World Writing Quarterly*.

Cornerstone Contributors' Notes

Adebola Adenle is a current senior at Carver Center for the Arts and Technology, as a literary arts magnet student. She deeply enjoys commentary videos and video essays, as well as anime and artistic gymnastics. Looking towards the future, Adebola seeks to pursue biochemical studies while retaining her literary studies and voice.

A Miami native, **Eva Alcaraz-Monje** is a senior at Lafayette High School located in Lexington, Kentucky. Eva is a member of the School for the Creative and Performing Arts (SCAPA) program, majoring in literary arts. Eva was a finalist for the 2024 Lexington Youth Poet Laureate and a first-place winner of the 2024 Kentucky State Poetry Society Student Poetry Contest, and has participated in the Young Writers Project at the Carnegie Center. Eva loves writing, especially horror, poetry, and journalism. When not at school or writing, you can find Eva by the creek near her house, hanging around downtown Lexington with friends, or lost in a Michaels.

Jack DeBoyace is an emerging poet from Pennsylvania. His poetry has been published in *The Bucks County Herald* and *Writes of Passage*. He placed first runner-up in the 2024 Bucks County High School Poet of the Year competition. At school, Jack serves as the entertainment editor for his school newspaper, *The Patriot Newspaper*, and edits for *Bridgework*, a creative writing literary magazine he founded at his high school.

Clara Dekker is a junior located in Lexington, Kentucky. She is an avid animal lover who has been writing since the age of nine. Outside of poetry and fiction, Clara takes an interest in music and baking. You can find her published book *Rising Dawn (Herds of the Wild)* on Amazon.

Pharaoh Jones is a Twin Cities-based writer, actor, and martial artist. He has been getting back into the groove of writing consistent poetry as of this last summer, but has always enjoyed writing. His poetry is often inspired by his acting experiences, stories of biking, and more often than not, nature. He is a junior at the Saint Paul Conservatory for Performing Artists, specializing in theater.

Jovina Zion Pradeep is the 2024–25 Alameda County Youth Poet Laureate, an editor at *Blossomer Literary Magazine* and at *Polyphony Lit*. Her work is published in *Tri City Voice*, *Moonstone Arts Center New Voices Anthology*, *San Francisco Youth Anthology*, *The Howl*, *SeaGlass Literary*, and *The Dungeness Press*. When she is not writing, taking photographs, or studying, you can find her singing, reading mythology, or listening to music.

A senior in high school, **Erika Prasthofer** is an emerging writer and poet. She is a winner of the 2024 Utah Poetry Ourselves competition and the 2023 Salt Lake City Public Library Teen Poetry Contest, and has been a recipient of three regional Scholastic awards. Her work has been published in her Salt Lake City high school's literary magazine, *Tesserae*, for which she has also been an editor.

Sophie Watson is a Kentucky-born, queer, young-adult writer. She enjoys writing confessionalist, free verse poetry and writes a poem daily, planning to continue this practice for the rest of her life. A senior at Lafayette High School, she is enrolled in the School for the Creative and Performing Arts program, majoring in literary arts. She enjoys all art forms and aspires to publish her first poetry book before turning nineteen.

www.ingramcontent.com/pod-product-compliance
Lightning Source LLC
LaVergne TN
LVHW041813060526
838201LV00046B/1244